"Compellingly belie[...]
DOORS, TURN ON [...]
THE HOUSE AND E[...]
South Be[...]

IF I SHOULD DIE

IF I SHOULD DIE

M.R. HENDERSON

AVON
PUBLISHERS OF BARD, CAMELOT, DISCUS AND FLARE BOOKS

AVON BOOKS
A division of
The Hearst Corporation
1790 Broadway
New York, New York 10019

The Doubleday edition contains the following Library of Congress Cataloging
in Publication Data:

Henderson, M.R.
    If I should die.
    I. Title.
PS3558.E48714   1985   813'.54   84-18785

First Avon Printing: July 1986

For Herb Kastle, friend and mentor unsurpassed,
and of course, for Morrice

Now I lay me down to sleep;
I pray the Lord my soul to keep.
If I should die before I wake,
I pray the Lord my soul to take.

A Child's Prayer,
The New England Primer, 1781

IF I SHOULD DIE

1

Motionless, he watched the cabin. A light had come on, and from time to time shadows moved behind the curtains, but everything was quiet. No radio, no television, no voices to break the morning stillness.

The light went off. He blinked as his gaze slid across the dark shadow of the building. Dawn had slithered into the morning sky, but the brooding pines wrapped the house in velvet gloom. Another light flicked on as a figure moved into view behind the yellow curtains.

His jaw ticked. It could be either of them. From this angle and distance he couldn't tell. No hurry. He was good at waiting.

He became aware of the sun working through the network of pines. In a few hours it would be sweat-hot, but now the promise of warmth was welcome. He was hungry, but he forced himself not to think about it. Suddenly the cabin door opened. He held his breath, as though the slight nasal sound of air escaping his lungs might drift downhill with the whispering breeze.

The woman ducked her head against the sudden burst of sunlight as she stepped out onto the tiny back porch. Her hair was pulled back in a ponytail. In blue jeans and a pink blouse, she looked about fifteen. His jaw ticked. He clenched his teeth.

As she reached the bottom step, a child ran out behind her. The man on the hill studied him curiously. Four or five . . . blond, like her. Did the kid have her eyes? Clear bluegreen, like the glass insulators he used to shoot off utility poles. The kid's laughter pierced the quiet. Opening a plastic bag, the woman helped the child scatter bread crumbs around the clearing. They were almost directly below him. Through the branches, he saw the neckline of her blouse fall open as she leaned forward. His fingers chewed into the tree bark as he glimpsed the dusky canyon between her breasts. Above him, a blue jay squawked skyward.

The boy looked up, pointing. The watcher shrank into the shadows when the woman shielded her eyes and gazed upward. He didn't let out his breath until she turned away. Grabbing a handful of crumbs, she twirled like a ballerina, letting them scatter. The boy awkwardly tried to imitate, making her laugh as she ducked from the sudden spray.

A man's voice broke the crystalline laughter. "Breakfast is ready. Come and get it!"

The watcher had been so intent on the woman, he hadn't seen the figure appear in the doorway. He narrowed his eyes to study him. Dark, curly hair. Dark eyes. Medium build. The watcher dismissed him, turning his attention back to the woman. She dumped the rest of the crumbs as the child ran to the house. She followed, almost gliding, with the sun glinting on her golden ponytail. At the doorway, the man slipped his arm around her waist. With his hand comfortably on the curve of her hip, they went inside.

Air scraped from the watcher's lungs. He winced as pain scorched his knuckles. Jerking his hand from the tree, he watched the bright droplets of blood ooze on his skin. Frowning, he put the hand to his mouth and sucked.

Slowly he lowered himself to a squat and settled down to wait.

2

"Are you sure you won't change your mind and go with me?" Elliot gave her one of those special smiles that reached deep inside to warm her.

Kay shook her head, hiding the doubt he'd read in her eyes if she wasn't careful. "We'll be fine. Stop worrying."

"I feel like a heel leaving you to pack—"

"I can handle it." She raised on tiptoes to kiss him. She and Jeff would be fine . . . when they got back from the airport, they'd be on their way in less than an hour. . . .

"You're sure? When I told Harriet I was going to New York, she offered to help. It'll take only a few minutes to go by her place and ask her to give you a hand." Harriet Sanderson was their nearest neighbor, two miles as the crow flew but five miles along the deep V of gravel roads that were the only connection between the two isolated cabins. Harriet was a strong, independent woman in her late fifties who'd retired to the Sierra when her husband died five years before.

"I'm positive," Kay insisted. "Go get your stuff. If you miss that plane after all this—" She shoved him playfully toward the bedroom. She wanted desperately to display a brave front, because she knew her inner fears wouldn't stand the scrutiny of close cross-examination. Normally Elliot would never consider going to New York without first helping her close up the cabin and drive back to Los Angeles. But he was due back at his job at the Los Angeles

Times in three days. Kay couldn't deny him the pleasure of launching his manuscript personally.

Elliot had worked straight through the past two weeks, pounding at the typewriter until she dragged him to bed. Even then he was back at work before she and Jeff stirred in the morning. Now he'd finished, and he was excited about the final draft. Excited enough to fly to New York and get an opinion from Trevor Rogers, his longtime friend and new literary agent. Kay approved wholeheartedly, sharing his excitement because she knew how much it meant to him. They'd opened a bottle of champagne to celebrate.

She hugged her arms across her breasts as she recalled the joyous lovemaking last night. It was only later with Elliot snoring softly beside her in the dark that she realized she'd be alone in the cabin after she dropped him at the airport. But it wouldn't be for long . . . she and Jeff would be back from Reno by nine. They could close up the cabin and be home in Los Angeles before dark if Jeff didn't demand too many pit stops.

Elliot emerged from the bedroom with his suitcase and the manuscript box sealed with heavy tape. Unconsciously he cradled it to his chest. His baby, she thought. It had taken longer to produce than a child. Almost two years. Was it elephants that carried their young that long? She thought about the months Elliot had slaved. The clack of the typewriter became such a steady rhythm, a mockingbird chattered it during momentary lulls. He'd worked mostly in Los Angeles, after his full-day stint at his newspaper job. She marveled at the fresh energy he'd been able to bring to his writing when most men would have been content to flop in front of the television and sate their brains with mindless fare until bedtime. He'd been able to devote himself full time to the work only these last two weeks at the cabin.

"Let's go," Elliot said, heading for the door. "Come on, Tiger, there's an airplane waiting for me."

Jeff spread his arms and ran toward the door. "Vroom! I'm an airplane!" The screen door slammed behind him as he jumped down the steps, grabbing his Dodgers baseball cap when it slid off. He tugged at the car door.

"Hurry, Daddy—"

Elliot bounded down the steps two at a time. Smiling, Kay shut the cabin door and tested the lock before crossing the clearing to the car. She laughed when Elliot asked if she wanted him to drive.

"Not on your life. You'd have to let go of the manuscript, and that would put you in a state unfit for driving."

Grinning, Elliot gave her an affectionate kiss on the tip of the nose. He opened the car door for Jeff, then tossed his suitcase in back before climbing in beside Kay, still hugging the box. Jeff bounced impatiently.

"An airplane! An airplane!"

"Simmer down, honey," Kay scolded gently.

Jeff threw his arms around his father's neck and hugged him. "Can I fly in an airplane, Daddy?"

"Not this time, Tiger, but someday. When Daddy's book sells, we'll go on a real vacation."

"In an airplane?" Jeff started to bounce again.

"Yup." Elliot tousled Jeff's blond hair. "Now sit down and buckle your seat belt, okay?"

Jeff sat back, chattering happily to himself.

Careful not to flood the engine, Kay started the car and let it warm up. The marker on the highway said the elevation was 7000 feet, but that didn't include the steep grade up the logging road. Sierra nights were sharp year around, and the '78 Olds station wagon was temperamental. Satisfied with the smooth hum, she backed around the clearing and headed down the rutted trail.

On the hillside, the watcher cocked his head as the sound of the car hovered in the clear morning. When at last it was quiet, he got up slowly and stretched his stiff muscles.

3

Kay set the emergency brake and glanced at the dappled shadows that played across the front of the cabin. With Elliot gone, everything seemed different, as though he'd packed the sunshine in his suitcase and left behind a cold imitation of light. The trees were a tightening knot of dark uniformed guards around the clearing. She shivered. Elliot's plane had taken off only an hour ago, and here she was looking for ghosts in broad daylight. How was she going to survive three days without him? With difficulty, she thought wryly. First thing, she had to banish the boogeyman in the shadows. Resolutely she snapped the switch to unlock the car doors.

"Let's get rolling," she said to Jeff. "We'll pack the car and be on our way faster than you can say 'Scoobie Doo.' "

Jeff tumbled out. She grabbed him as he started for the cabin. "Whoa. You carry the cookies." She'd found a 7-11 open and bought bread, cookies, and doughnuts. She'd make sandwiches, fill a thermos with coffee, and put a plastic bottle of orange juice in the cooler so they could have a picnic lunch at a roadside rest where Jeff could run off some energy.

Jeff clutched the bag as he skipped across the clearing, his four-year-old enthusiasm directed toward the new adventure of returning to Los Angeles. Kay dug in her purse for the house keys, glancing at her watch. Ten to nine.

6

They could still make Los Angeles before dark. Suddenly she wanted to be in the city, with neighbors nearby, in the familiar house that was saturated with the new life she and Elliot had built. She longed for Elliot. In six years, he'd changed her life so completely, the past was almost erased. Almost. Just as she couldn't change the past, neither could she forget it completely, much as she tried. It was better now than it had been at first, thanks to Elliot and Jeff. Old ghosts came only in odd moments when she was alone . . . missing Elliot . . . here at the isolated cabin she'd never gotten used to. She shook away the gloomy thoughts.

Jeff scooted past as she opened the door. He tossed the cookie sack on the sofa and darted for his room. Smiling, Kay let him go. On the drive back from Reno, she'd told him they had to pack up and leave as fast as possible. She'd probably have to repack everything he tossed into his bag, but he was eager to help. He didn't look unhappy about leaving. Maybe he was glad to go too. Or maybe he was picking up on her fear. Elliot always warned her: "Kids tune in on your feelings. It's no good saying there's nothing to be afraid of if you jump at every shadow."

She set the grocery sacks on the kitchen counter, then got a chair so she could reach the Styrofoam cooler on top of the cupboard. Checking the refrigerator, she took out cheese and leftover roast beef for sandwiches.

Jeff's head poked in the doorway. "Mommy, can I take my flippers?"

"Sure." They probably wouldn't be back up. After Labor Day, the weather was unpredictable. She hated the moaning wind and the crunching leaves and pine needles. The leaves fell early at this elevation, as though eager to escape the relentless approach of winter.

She opened the freezer and groaned when she saw the empty ice cube trays. She'd forgotten to fill them last night after dumping ice into Jeff's plastic beach pail for a make-shift champagne bucket. Jeff would have to drink his orange juice lukewarm unless she stopped someplace for cubes. Unwrapping the cheese and meat, she began to make sandwiches. She had three stacked and was cutting them when she heard a floorboard behind her creak.

Without turning, she said, "Did you look under the bed for dirty socks? And don't forget your swimsuit on the—"

"Hello, Katie."

The butcher knife trembled in her hand as she whirled around.

"You look great, Katie. Aren't you glad to see me?"

When he stepped toward her she cringed. His gaze flicked to her hand, and she realized she was still holding the butcher knife. She brought it up quickly, instinctively, pointing the gleaming, sharp tip between them. Catlike, he sprang and grabbed her arm, slamming it against the counter. The knife clattered to the floor. He kicked it aside, still holding her wrist.

"Don't make me mad, Katie."

The words sucked her through a wrinkle in the fabric of the past . . . *"Don't make me mad, Katie." Oh, God, don't let him get mad.* She tried to pull away as his arm slid around her, but he gripped her tightly, tangling one hand in her ponytail and forcing her head back. He clamped his mouth on hers. The brutal pressure made her whimper. Her throat filled with bile as his wet tongue forced between her teeth.

"I dreamed about this so long, Katie." He leaned against her, so close she felt his breath on her face. The edge of the counter dug at her spine but she didn't feel the pain as he kissed her again.

It isn't happening . . . it can't be . . . he can't be here! In a minute she'd wake up and turn off the alarm. The nightmare would end. Elliot would be in bed beside her and Jeff asleep in his room—

Jeff—She quivered with a cold wash of terror.

Matt's arm tightened. "You missed me, too, didn't you, Katie? I promised I'd come back. Don't I always come back?"

A puppet controlled by fear, she nodded, not in answer but appeasement. She needed time to think. Where was Jeff? Suppose he came bursting in—

"You surprised me, Matt," she finally managed to say. "How—did you get out?"

He laughed like a child with a secret. "Walked out and drove away, just like that."

"They gave you parole?" She was shaking so hard she was afraid the words would chatter against each other.

The smile vanished in the peculiar way he had of changing expression without warning. His gray eyes glinted like an arctic sea under the winter sun. His jaw ticked.

"The stupid parole board turned me down again. Said I couldn't come up for another three years." His face twisted. For a moment his fingers tightened and pain seared her arm. Then he let go abruptly and began pacing, knocking over one of the captain's chairs by the table and sending it crashing into the refrigerator with a furious kick.

Kay flexed her hand, not daring to take her eyes from him. She had to get him out of here—away from Jeff— away from her. She glanced at the butcher knife half hidden under the table, but before she could move, Matt whirled and strode back, his eyes wild.

"You know what it's like being locked up that way. I couldn't take it anymore."

He'd escaped. Oh, God—It had been years since that possibility had been part of her nightmares. He'd been in prison eleven years. For the first five, she'd been behind bars too, living a gray procession of days as she tried to forget the past and Matt Briggs. Even after her parole, nightmares left her sobbing and shaking at the thought Matt would get out and force his way back into her life. Bit by bit, Elliot's love and reassurances had soothed those fears until she felt secure. But now the nightmare was real. Matt was back. Here. Now.

When the parole board turned down Briggs's first appeal three years ago, Elliot had shown her the wire service story.

NO PAROLE FOR MAD DOG MATT

Soledad, Calif, (UPI)—Convicted mass slayer Matt
Briggs has been denied parole by state corrections officials in his bid for release from Soledad prison. The
parole board declined to set a release date for Briggs,
who now has served eight years of a life sentence.

The three-member board, which deliberated 35 minutes before making its unanimous decision, said the
next parole hearing for Briggs would be in 1984. The
board issued a statement that the denial was based on
the enormity of Briggs's crime and his prison record.
It refused to comment on the pressure being exerted
by the families of Briggs's victims and several church-
sponsored groups to keep "Mad Dog Matt" behind
bars "for the good of society."

The People's Coalition for Decency, a Stockton-
based organization, also demonstrated two years ago
against the release of Kathy Gerrett, Briggs's teenage
companion on his three-week robbery and murder
spree. Gerrett served five years in the Women's Correctional Institution at Frontera after being convicted
of complicity. Gerrett's release came two weeks after
her twenty-first birthday. Throughout her trial and imprisonment, Gerrett denied knowing that Briggs had
killed her father and young brother in a Blue Canyon,
Oregon, farmhouse before she accompanied him on a
six-state rampage that left a trail of blood in its wake.

Matt was staring at her with that frozen look she'd seen
in her nightmares. In his thin face, his gray eyes were
sockets in a bleached skull.

"I couldn't take it, Katie." He was suddenly childlike
and pleading. "You know, don't you?"

Her tongue stumbled in the dry canyon of her mouth.
"How did you find me?"

He gave a sly smile. "I know all about you, Katie. Everything."

The morning heat seemed to vanish. Kay shivered. "You —can't stay here. They'll be looking for you. They'll come here first thing." The media would rake over the past and dredge her life from obscurity, expose her to every front page across the country again. Rage filled her. How dare Matt Briggs come back! That part of her life was over. He had no right—

"Yeah, you're right," Matt said. "Let's go."

She shook her head, refusing to accept his words as she watched him pace with the jerky rhythm of a marionette. He raked his fingers through the ginger-colored hair that fell against the collar of his plaid shirt. For the first time, she realized he wasn't in prison clothes. He was wearing blue jeans that were too big, bunched under a leather belt that dangled a long end past a crudely punched notch. Over the shirt, a threadbare brown cardigan left his bony wrists exposed.

"Come on," he said irritably. "You said they'd come here first!"

Kay clutched the counter as her knees buckled. "I can't. I—I'm married and—"

He spun around so fast she stumbled back. He grabbed her, his fingers gouging her flesh. She gritted her teeth to keep from crying out.

"You said you'd wait!" Spurts of his breath slapped her face.

"T-that was a long time ago, Matt. Things have changed." He was insane to think she'd have any part of him. She tried to pull away, but he shook her like a rag doll, rattling her teeth and bouncing her ponytail against her shoulders.

"You said always. Always is forever!"

Tears scalded her cheeks and she tasted salty blood where she'd bitten her lip. Consumed by terror, she tried to think. She couldn't go with him. The idea made her physically ill. Her whole life was at stake. Resentment and rage made her sob.

Matt cocked his head, studying her for a moment, then taking her in his arms, his fury spent. "It'll be like old times, Katie. It was good then. It'll be good again, you'll see. So many things we didn't have time to do. We'll do them now"

"Mommy?"

Kay jerked up. Matt pinned her between his arms as he looked around. In the doorway, Jeff's puzzled expression was accusing. "You said to hurry."

Kay licked her lips. "Take your things out to the car—"

Matt pushed away abruptly. Kay took a quick step, but her legs went rubbery as he scooped up the butcher knife from the floor, then knelt by Jeff.

"Hi, kid."

Jeff looked at the knife warily. His hazel eyes were solemn, as though he hadn't yet made up his mind about the stranger who'd made his mother cry.

"You like to fish?"

Jeff nodded.

"Maybe I'll take you fishing."

Kay pressed her hand to her lips. Matt balanced the knife on his outstretched palm. She was aware of his sidelong glance.

"You wanna go fishing?" Matt persisted.

Jeff's gaze sought his mother, then settled on the tips of his worn tennis shoes, as though he sensed the danger in any answer he might give.

"I said, you wanna go fishing?" Matt's voice was querulous. When Jeff didn't answer, Matt flipped the knife like a juggler and stabbed Jeff's chest with the blunt handle. "Answer me, dummy!" Jeff cringed.

Kay sobbed, "Matt, please!" Frightened, Jeff looked at her to correct whatever had gone wrong with their morning. She tried to reassure him with a smile, but her face was stiff and unresponsive. "It's okay, Jeff. Matt is—Matt is someone I knew a long time ago. He came to"—she swallowed—"to say hello. Be nice to him, okay?" *Oh, God, don't make him mad. . . .*

Matt's anger was appeased as Jeff gave him an obedient smile, his doubts suspended. "That's more like it. We're gonna get along fine, me and you. We're gonna be pals." He stood abruptly and looked at Kay. "Get the car keys."

She moved uncertainly, trying to put herself between him and Jeff. Matt waved the knife.

"The keys—the keys!"

"Matt, please—"

Matt examined the edge of the blade with his thumb. "Damn it, don't make me mad, Katie. Get the keys."

4

No matter how you did it, you lost an entire day flying West to East Coast. Elliot cursed the long flight and the time difference that put him in a cab from JFK at the peak of rush hour. If it were anyone but Trevor, he'd have to wait until morning. But he and Trevor Rogers had been friends before Elliot ever thought of writing a novel or Trevor of becoming a New York literary agent. They'd both worked under Wayne Sanderson on the L. A. *Times* back when they were newly graduated from journalism school and eager to set the world on fire. Together they moaned about the lost-kid and found-wallet stories they were assigned, and they dreamed about the big chance that would get them by-lines and Pulitzers.

Elliot watched the stream of traffic on the other side of the expressway. Maybe Trevor was smart, getting out when he did. Maybe he should have gotten out then, too, and written his book. He could be living on the south coast of France, sipping champagne and eating caviar. But he hadn't. And because he hadn't, his life was enriched by Kay and Jeff. He smiled at his reflection in the dusty window. Kay and Jeff gave purpose and meaning to success. The champagne and caviar would be the better for sharing it with them.

A frown worried his brow as he remembered the uneasiness Kay hadn't been able to disguise when she kissed him good-bye. She was scared, no matter what she said.

He cursed himself for ten kinds of a louse for not getting her and Jeff back to Los Angeles before taking off. But with the book done, he'd been jumping around like a kid with a new puppy. What did he expect her to say?

He'd call her as soon as he got to Trevor's. Damn. She wouldn't even be home yet. He'd flown across the country in less time than she could drive from the cabin to Los Angeles. It was a hard trip with no one to spell you at the wheel. And he knew damned well she'd never stay overnight in a motel, no matter what she said. They rarely talked about the past anymore, but Elliot knew Kay's joy in being a wife and mother didn't completely obliterate dark memories that stirred occasionally. Maybe it never would, but she'd come so far, no one would know she was the same frightened kid who'd made national headlines eleven years ago.

His first glimpse of Kathy Gerrett had been as she was led to a sheriff's car in Kern County. She was pale and drawn, with dark shadows under her blue, terror-filled eyes. Her blond hair was limp across a soiled red cashmere sweater.

Elliot had been en route to the cabin for a long weekend when he heard a radio bulletin that Mad Dog Matt Briggs had been captured in Barstow after a grocery store holdup that left two dead and another critical with knife wounds. Briggs defiantly refused to tell where his girl friend was. No one expected her to be a hundred miles away. Briggs had never ranged that far from his lair before.

When two highway patrol cars roared past at seventy miles an hour, Elliot made a U-turn and followed with a reporter's instinct that paid off. The sheriff's men surrounded a rural farmhouse with guns drawn and megaphones booming. A wizened old duffer walked out with his hands high, followed by a girl who couldn't stop crying long enough to put her hands in the air. Kathy Gerrett had knocked on the door of the farmhouse and asked the old man to call the sheriff. Sobbing, she said Briggs had threatened to kill her if she tried to get away while he was gone. When she heard a bulletin about his capture on the radio, she finally found the courage to leave the desert shack where they'd been hiding.

The sheriff cuffed her and passed a length of chain between her hands. Two brawny officers grabbed the ends as if walking a wild panther. As Elliot raised his Nikon for a series of quick, candid shots, his gaze met the girl's, and he thought of a wounded fawn, dazed and unable to comprehend the pain that had been thrust on her. When she was rushed into a waiting car, Elliot joined the caravan back to town. The first choppers were on the courthouse lawn, spewing reporters who'd heard the alert, news vultures sniffing the scent of new blood. While they crowded into the sheriff's office, Elliot phoned in the story from a booth. The *Times* bannered it in the late edition before the rest of the reporters had their notes deciphered.

Kathy Gerrett had given him his big break. No Pulitzer, but a by-line and a shot at covering the trial. The follow-up after her imprisonment had been his own idea. Somehow he hadn't been able to forget the expression in her eyes when she walked out of that farmhouse. Throughout the trial and sentencing, he couldn't shake the haunting feeling maybe it had happened the way she said, despite Briggs's testimony she'd been his willing accomplice.

The cab came out of Central Park and turned north. Elliot dug out his wallet as he glanced at the meter, then his watch. Even if Kay and Jeff had gotten off right away, they wouldn't be home for another four hours, maybe three and a half. He'd call her after dinner. Maybe Trevor would have the manuscript read by then.

Trevor Rogers lived on the eighteenth floor of a West Side tower overlooking the park. The view reminded Elliot of the Hollywood Hills—green bathed in a shimmering Monet haze by daylight and black satin pinpointed by diamond lights at night. It still amazed him that Trevor had adjusted so well to the Big Apple. In spite of the rat race, Trevor had never lost his laid-back California aura.

There were four apartment entrances off the tiny hall that housed the elevator. Alerted by the doorman downstairs, Trevor had his door open in welcome. Elliot set his suitcase in the hall.

"In here," Trevor called. Tall and slender, with hair graying prematurely at the temples, he looked comfortable in slacks and a sport shirt as he stood at a liquor cart putting together two martinis. He grinned as he held out a glass. "It's the only antidote for a ride from Kennedy."

"You can say that again. Here's looking at you, old buddy."

Trevor indicated the rust corduroy sofa. "Relax. I presume that's the manuscript you're clutching?"

Elliot grinned sheepishly. "Now that the moment of truth is at hand, I'm scared."

Trevor laughed. "Come on, Elliot, none of that bullshit. We both know you can write, so it's just a matter of whether or not you've got a salable novel. You use the same tools for journalism and fiction. Only the format's different."

"You sound like an agent."

Trevor nodded. "Your agent, if you've got what I think you have."

Elliot put the box on the coffee table. Trevor was right. It was time for the damned thing to solo. Either it flew or it didn't. He finished his drink, but when Trevor started to get up, he gestured.

"Let me. I'm tired of sitting." He carried the glasses to the bar as Trevor began to slit open the tape sealing the box. "How's the agency going?" Elliot was amazed at the sudden butterflies in his stomach. "Last I heard, you were taking in a girl to help. How'd it go?"

Trevor slid a pocketknife along a seam. "Fantastic. I took her right out of college, and she's got what it takes. I trust her first readings. She's already handling a couple of clients who are doing romances. The trouble is, I'll get her broken in just right and she'll run off and open her own agency.''

''Make her a partner.''

''After eight years of building the business single-handed? Not on your life. It's easier to train a new one.''

''No wonder you aren't married.''

Trevor laughed. ''Speaking of which, how are Kay and Jeff?''

''Fine, but right now she's probably cussing me out like a truck driver who's been cut off on the approach to a long grade. I left her to pack up and drive back to L.A. alone with Jeff. He's at that fun age where his favorite question is, 'Are we there yet?' ''

''You should have brought them along. I haven't seen Kay since—in years.''

''Since her trial,'' Elliot said matter-of-factly. ''You wouldn't know her. She's a beautiful woman, not a scared kid anymore.''

''I'm glad everything worked out. I made some pretty stupid remarks when you told me you were going to marry her.''

''Water under the bridge.'' Elliot brought back two frosty martinis. Trevor hadn't been alone in predicting disaster for the marriage. Long ago Elliot had inured himself to the fact that Kathy Gerrett would be on trial forever in the minds of the public. Even close friends like Trevor and the Sandersons had given their blessings to the marriage hesitantly. Already in New York, Trevor never had the chance to know Kay. When Harriet recovered from the shock of Wayne's death, she put aside her doubts about Kay's past and offered warm friendship.

Elliot settled with his drink and watched Trevor extract the manuscript from the box. Suddenly he wished he'd mailed the damn thing. Trevor raised his glass in a toast and smiled.

"What do you say I read a couple of chapters before we go out to dinner? It'll give us something to talk about."

"Sounds good." Elliot sipped his martini, studying Trevor's face for subtle reactions as he read. At least he was absorbed, Elliot thought. That was a good sign.

After some minutes, the phone rang, and Trevor reached for it without looking up. When his initial "Yes?" was answered, he looked surprised. His gaze found Elliot. "I think you'd better talk to him," he told the caller. He held the receiver out to Elliot. "It's Harriet Sanderson."

Elliot grabbed the phone. "Harriet? Has something happened? Are Kay and Jeff all right?"

"No—yes. Damn it, I'm a fool for scaring you this way, Elliot, I'm sorry."

Relieved, he sat back. "What's up?"

"I knew you were on the plane all day, so I figured you haven't heard. It hasn't hit the national news yet."

"What hasn't?"

"Matt Briggs escaped from Soledad yesterday."

"What!"

"They think he got over to the honor farm somehow with a batch of transferees, then just walked away."

"That's crazy! You don't just walk away from Soledad." Fear swelled uncontrollably and exploded as anger.

Harriet's tone was empathetic. "I thought you'd want to come back to be with Kay."

My God—Kay! "I'll catch the first plane to L.A. Harriet, do me a favor? Drive over to the cabin and make sure she and Jeff got off okay?"

"I heard the car a little after nine, but I'll be glad to go over if it will ease your mind."

"Thanks." When he cradled the phone, his hand was shaking.

Trevor whistled softly. "There wasn't anything on the six o'clock news. They may have picked him up already."

Elliot nodded absently. Briggs's picture had been in every newspaper and magazine eleven years ago. If he hadn't already been caught, he was probably a long way from California. But, like Harriet, Elliot was worried about Kay. With Briggs on the run, she'd be frightened. And the press would drag the whole story back to the front page. The past he and Kay wanted to forget would resurface like a bloated corpse.

Trevor picked up the phone. "I'll have someone get you on the first flight."

Elliot paced, staring out the window, not seeing the park but Kathy Gerrett's frightened, drawn face as she walked out of that farmhouse eleven years ago.

5

Harriet Sanderson's jeep spat a thick plume of dust as blue jays protested the alien intrusion on the mountainside. Harriet squinted against the gritty cloud that billowed around the jeep and hung in the still air. It hadn't rained for two months. The ground was parched and the pines wore a dull, gray film. Despite the hard winter with above-average snowfall, the hot, dry summer had left the forest tinder dry. She breathed a sigh of relief that they'd gotten through the tourist season without any devastating fires. Tourists tended to be more careless than natives, whose houses and businesses were at risk, not to mention their lives.

Harriet hated the tourists. It seemed impossible that she had been one when she fell in love with the High Sierra country. She was so much a part of it now, she claimed it as fiercely as a patriot. She had trouble seeing herself in the life she'd once led in Los Angeles. Except for Wayne. In the past five years his memory hadn't dimmed, only become less painful. She was over her rage at his death and the senseless loss of a man in his prime. A man who taught her to love people and places, and who had first brought her here.

"Breathe the air, Harriet," he'd said. "Smell it? That's freedom. A body can live out here and grow without stepping on everyone else's feet doing it. What would you say to moving up here?"

21

Smiling, she'd answered, "You retire? Newspapering is the air you breathe."

He shook his head. "There's a side a man doesn't show to the rest of the world much. I love my work, but I love freedom more. I need it." He looked at her with such yearning, she felt a surge of tenderness. When she put her hand on his arm, he covered it with his broad, blunt fingers. "The city's getting me, Harriet. I'm tired. Old."

"You're not old!"

"I will be if I stay in Los Angeles much longer. What would you say to buying a small paper up here somewhere? Run it. Live in the woods. Just the two of us."

"I'd say, 'Why not, Wayne Sanderson? You deserve it.' "

"You mean that, Harriet?"

She nodded, knowing she had to give him the chance to fulfill his dream, but also certain he'd tire of it and go back to the rat race he thought he wanted to escape. They'd come back on weekends while he snooped around the tiny towns that dotted the Sierra. Many were too small to support a newspaper; others merited a second look. He finally found one that showed promise. It was a one-man paper published out of a printing office, but the potential was there. Wayne began talking terms with the owner.

Before it was settled, he was gone. No warning, no reprieves, no second chance. A swift and deadly heart attack felled him at his desk at the Los Angeles *Times*. His dream was wiped out in an instant. And Harriet's life as well, or so it seemed for a long time. She drifted from day to day like smoke on an autumn breeze, without purpose or desire. And one day when the pain was too much to bear, she'd gotten in the car and driven north, where at last she found peace among the tall pines and crisp air Wayne had called freedom.

Now, as she thought about Elliot and Kay, a new ache crowded her heart. Such nice young kids with so much to look forward to in life. Damn it, she hoped Briggs was

picked up fast. The sooner the story of his escape disappeared from the news, the faster Kay would be able to
recapture the peace of being Mrs. Elliot Pier instead of
Kathy Gerrett, former accomplice of Mad Dog Matt.

Had Kay heard the news bulletin? There were long
stretches of the San Joaquin Valley where radio reception
was poor. Kay might not twist the dial for local stations if
Jeff was sleeping. Harriet smiled, thinking of Jeff. A bundle of energy. Bright and inquisitive, too. She loved him
as much as she would the grandchild she and Wayne never
had.

The jeep bounced onto the rough trail leading to the Pier
cabin. In the clearing, she shifted into neutral and glanced
at the oil stain where the Olds was usually parked. She let
out a relieved sigh that Kay had gotten off. She wondered
if she should call Elliot back before he left New York and
put his mind at ease.

She shifted gears and made a tight circle in front of the
porch steps, then hit the brake, frowning. Looking back,
she geared into neutral and set the hand brake. She walked
back and picked up a swim fin lying in the grass. It was
Jeff's. A flutter of movement drew her glance to an open
window where the curtain was blowing behind the screen.

Worried, she climbed the steps, her head tilted as she
listened for voices over the soft purr of the jeep's idling
engine. Turning the knob, she let the door swing inward.

"Kay?"

Silence.

"Kay? Yoo-hoo, it's Harriet."

Silence.

The living room had a deserted air rather than the closed-
at-the-end-of-the-season finality. Jeff's other swim fin lay
on a chintz chair. Beside it was a duffel bag with a striped
sock poking from the zippered top. Beyond an open door,
she saw Jeff's unmade bed with a box of toys on it. She
went down the hall to the other bedroom. The covers were
thrown back on the king-size bed. A partially packed suit-

case was on it. The open closet door revealed dresses and sweaters hung in a neat row. Through the open bathroom door, she saw Kay's hair dryer and cosmetics on the sink. Fear gnawing, Harriet went to the kitchen.

She stared at the untidy counter littered with bread crumbs, flecks of meat, and a smear of mayonnaise. The jar stood uncapped, a roll of wax paper beside it. Harriet opened the refrigerator. A jar of olives and a dish covered with plastic wrap. Harriet worried her lip. Kay had taken off in a hurry. Because of the news broadcast? Walking through the rooms once more, Harriet found the radio alarm clock beside the bed and put her hand on it like a psychic summoning kinetic vibrations. If Kay heard Matt Briggs was on the loose, she might panic and run. Without her clothes? Without locking the door? Was it possible she was coming back?

A new thought struck. Harriet returned to the bathroom and scrutinized it for any sign that Jeff or Kay had been sick or hurt. The first aid kit was intact in the medicine cabinet. Back in the living room, Harriet glanced around speculatively. Something had happened, that was certain, Kay and Elliot had closed up the cabin often enough to follow the procedure by rote: pack clothes, strip the beds, spread dust sheets, empty the refrigerator, clean up all traces of food to discourage mice, bolt the windows and lock the doors.

Harriet knew she wasn't mistaken about hearing the car earlier. And the Olds was gone. One thing sure, she wasn't going to find any answers standing here. Outside, she knelt and reached under the porch. The spare key was where it always hung for her use or for Clem Daniels when he came to turn off the water and drain the pipes. She went back inside and checked the bolt on the rear door, then fastened all the windows before letting herself out and locking up. She replaced the key, then climbed back into the jeep. She'd call Clem to see if Kay had contacted him.

By the time she got home, she'd changed her mind half

a dozen times about calling Elliot back. Instead she called
the Truckee hospital. Neither Kay nor Jeff had been admitted. She phoned Dr. Mensiller's office with the same
results. As a last resort, she phoned Ed Viemont at the
Sierra Press.

"How have you been, Harriet? I've been meaning to get
up your way and say hello."

"I'm fine, Ed, but I have a problem."

"What can I do to help?" The first time Ed and Wayne
had met they'd forged a special friendship of men who
understand each other. Even though the sale of the paper
had never materialized, Ed had grieved with Harriet at
Wayne's death, and he'd welcomed her back to the Sierra
with warm, dependable friendship. During the summer
months when the *Press* came out twice a week, they saw
little of each other unless Harriet happened to be in town
and stopped by the printing office. But when fall thinned
the leaves and tourists, they made a point of having dinner
once a week.

"This is off the record, Ed."

"Whatever you say. You sound worried."

She'd never discussed Kay's past with anyone. Elliot,
Jeff, and Kay were her family, and she'd never betray their
trust.

"I guess I am a little." Quickly she sketched the essen-
tials of Kay's hasty departure, emphasizing how out of
character it was.

"She probably changed her mind about closing up and
went to Reno or Sacramento for the day," Ed offered.

"She wouldn't drive over to my place without locking
the door. Frankly, I'm concerned. I called her doctor and
the hospital, but she hasn't been at either."

"You say she was planning to head for L.A.?"

"Definitely."

"You want me to check with the highway patrol?"

"Would you? I'd feel a lot better."

"I'll call you back in twenty minutes."

"Thanks, Ed."

"Sure, now stop worrying. There's usually a simple explanation for these things. Some old friend probably came by unexpectedly and she's off having a good time."

Harriet hung up and scowled at her oval face with its soft cap of gray hair in the antique mirror above the fireplace. Ed's parting remark had stirred a sense of dread. That was exactly what she was worried about, only Matt Briggs wasn't a friend. He was a deadly threat. Her clear amber eyes stared back at her. Wait. Wait for Ed's call.

Restlessly, she moved around the room, then snapped on the radio. Reception was poor, but a local station had a strong enough signal to climb the hill, albeit accompanied by static and fading. Glancing at the clock, she knew it would be fifteen minutes until a scheduled newscast unless there was a bulletin. She resisted the temptation to twist the dial in search of an errant signal and forced herself to wait. When the broadcast came, there was no further news on the escape. Harriet sank into the wing chair near the window. She was worrying about nothing. There'd be a simple explanation as Ed predicted. When the phone rang, she raced for it.

"You can stop worrying, Harriet," he said without preamble. "I had Johnny Pouli run a check through the state computer. The highway patrol has no report of an accident or breakdown. Those boys are pretty much on top of things, so they should know. I also asked the Reno police to check their hospitals and emergency centers. Kay hasn't been there either."

"That's a relief." Fishing, she improvised. "Do you know of anything that might have spooked her? Storm warnings, maybe?"

"Don't we wish. The weatherman says more of the same. Hot and dry. Why do I get the feeling you're holding back, Harriet? Have you got something specific on your mind?"

She hesitated. "I heard a newscast earlier about that killer who escaped from Soledad. If there was any reason to think he might be headed this way, it would be enough to scare the wits out of a young mother alone with a four-year-old.'' She heard Ed shuffle papers.

"Matt Briggs. Yeah, I heard it, but Soledad's a long way from here. Any reason he should head this way?"

"I'm grasping at straws."

"Okay, I'll check. Guess I'd be remiss in my duties as an honest journalist not to follow up on the story. I'll get back to you, Harriet. You going to be home?"

"I'll be here."

Glancing at the clock, she wondered if Elliot was en route to Los Angeles. Telling him her fears would only add to his own, and what the devil could he do thirty thousand feet over mid-America? And maybe there *was* nothing to worry about. Maybe Kay and Jeff would be in the Hollywood house when Elliot got there.

Harriet tried to imagine Kay's reaction if she'd heard the news of Briggs's escape. Kay loved Elliot so fiercely, she pretended to enjoy the cabin as much as he, but Harriet sensed the apprehension behind Kay's darting glances at the woods and the way she wrapped her arms around herself whenever she was outside alone. It was as if she saw phantoms in the shadows, phantoms of the terror-filled weeks when Matt Briggs had dragged her from one isolated spot to another. If there was the remotest chance Briggs was around, Kay would bolt for the sprawling anonymity and safety of the city.

The phone rang. Harriet grabbed it. "Yes?"

"I didn't have any trouble picking up a report on Briggs," Ed said. "I think I'll hire you on as a news hound."

"What do you mean?" She pressed a hand against her heart's wild beat.

"He's headed this way, all right. The laundry truck he stole in Soledad was found in Coalinga. They thought he was heading south until a farmer got around to reporting that one of his pickups has been missing since yesterday. His Mexicans had it out in the fields. When they missed it, they figured the bossman had driven it back.''

''And?'' she prompted, unable to keep her hand from trembling.

''It was found a little while ago in Yuba City. The highway patrol thinks there may be a connection. They're setting up roadblocks.''

Harriet's breath caught.

''Harriet? You okay?''

''Yes, thanks, Ed.''

''Harriet, Briggs is considered dangerous. This latest development hasn't been released to the media yet, so how could Kay Pier have heard it?'' Harriet's silence was long and tense. Finally Ed said, ''I think it's time for us to get together for dinner. I'll bring some steaks for the grill. About seven okay?''

She glanced at the clock. It was going to be a long afternoon. ''Come earlier if you can, Ed. I can use some company.''

6

At Matt's order, Kay wrapped the sandwiches and put them in the cooler with the orange juice and carried it out to the car. Jeff trailed after her, puzzled by her nervousness and the stranger's growing impatience, but eager to be under way. Matt picked up Kay's purse and went through it quickly. When she tried to get in back of the Olds with Jeff, Matt shoved the keys at her.

"You drive. And the kid sits between us so me and him can talk. In you go— What's your name anyhow?"

"Jeff." It was a brave overture of friendliness, even though the man still held the knife.

"Okay, Jeff, climb in." Matt waved the knife. Jeff moved quickly, not sure if the man's friendly tone or the knife was more important. Kay got behind the wheel. She was shaking so badly, she wasn't sure she could drive, but she was too scared to argue. Matt had never been a good driver. Ten years in prison wouldn't have improved him. And if she drove she'd be in control. She could steer the car off the road or attract attention . . .

"Get it started!" Matt ordered. He pulled Jeff close and kept one hand on his shoulder.

Kay twisted the key. She was in too much of a rush. *Don't stall it* . . . The warm engine responded immediately. She looked at Matt.

"Down to the highway, and don't try anything, you

hear?'' He laid the butcher knife across his leg, the tip pointing at Jeff.

She nodded, sickly aware of the dangerous thought she'd been considering. If she tried anything, he'd hurt Jeff before she could stop him. Carefully, she slipped the car in gear and made a tight circle in the clearing.

"Are we going fishing now?" Jeff asked eagerly, looking at Matt.

Kay was so startled, the wheel jerked in her hands and the car bumped in a rut. *Jeff didn't understand the danger. She had to warn him . . .*

Matt glanced around as though he'd forgotten Jeff was there. "What? No. Shut up."

Jeff's smile turned down at the corners. "I wanna go fishing."

Matt's hand clenched around the butcher knife. "Later. Now shut up, y'hear?"

Jeff hesitated, then retreated in disappointed silence. Kay let out her coiled breath as the moment of danger passed. She prayed Jeff would be quiet. She had to warn him not to consider Matt a friend, not to trust him for a moment. Nervously, she concentrated on the steep downgrade. When had Matt escaped? Were they looking for him? Had the police spread a wide net that might be closing in right now? She glanced furtively at the woods.

There was no sign of another car in the clearing or along the road. Had he come on foot? Was it the car he wanted? Where was he taking them? Questions that had no answers tortured her as she navigated down the logging road. When she reached the highway, Matt pointed east, toward Reno. She turned onto the interstate.

She was relieved to be on the main road, out of the brooding, isolated woods. Here the chance was better to attract attention and get help. Someone would notice. She'd driven this same road only a few hours ago, but the familiar landmarks blurred in her memory. *Elliot . . . oh, Elliot . . .*

As they approached the outskirts of Reno, Matt ordered her to stay at a sedate fifty-five miles an hour. "You try anything, the kid gets it. Understand?" He lifted the knife and flicked it across the leg of Jeff's cotton pants, nicking a small slit in the material. Jeff pulled away indignantly and pressed against Kay's hip. She reached out unsteadily to pat him and warn him to be quiet.

"I'll do what you say, only please don't frighten him anymore," she pleaded.

Matt laughed as if she'd said something funny. He let his hand slip down beside the door so the knife was hidden. Somehow it was more menacing unseen. Kay chanted Jeff's name silently to still her panic. Matt wouldn't hesitate to use Jeff to get what he wanted. Or the knife. Her stomach knotted convulsively. She took a quavering breath.

She hated Matt Briggs. He was part of the past with its horrible memories and shame. He had no right to come back into her life. It was a waking nightmare that couldn't be happening but that some small corner of her mind had always feared—known?—might come. She felt hot tears and wiped them away quickly.

Matt's total unconcern about pursuit worried her. Was he so sure of himself that he needed no apprehensive backward glances, no twisting the radio dial in search of news bulletins? Cold sweat dampened the nape of her neck. Except for curt instructions now and then, Matt was silent. The stillness inside the car was ominous, but she didn't dare break it for fear of prodding Matt's rage. He'd exploded so easily back at the cabin, she knew it could happen again any time. The memory of his violent, unpredictable moods surged from the depths of her mind like a chilling winter flood. *"Don't make me mad, Katie. . . ."*

In Reno, morning traffic had thinned to a sporadic trickle, and the Olds didn't attract any attention. Much too quickly, the city was behind them. Suddenly the road was unfamiliar, alien. Lonely. Panic began to seep through Kay

again. Who would miss her? With Elliot gone, no one
would go to the cabin. No one would know she wasn't on
her way to Los Angeles as planned. How long would it be
until Elliot realized something was wrong? Hours, maybe
not until tomorrow. She tried not to look at the clock on
the dashboard. Somehow knowing Elliot was blissfully en
route to New York made her and Jeff's predicament worse.

She had never been very far past Sparks before, and the
long stretch of barren high desert astonished her. Towns
were few and far between, set far back from the highway,
with only stark green and white exit markers to give cre-
dence to their existence. On either side, the arid, sun-
scorched rolling terrain merged into the distant blue haze
of mountains. An occasional car overtook them and sped
by; on the other side of the divided highway, traffic was
sparse.

Beside her, Jeff had retreated behind a wall of petulant
silence. Occasionally he glanced at Matt, but he didn't
speak to him again. He stared stonily ahead, as though
some warning signal emanated from the threatening
stranger. *Oh, Jeff, how can I make it up to you?*

When pain tightened Kay's shoulders, she realized she
was hunched over the wheel, gripping it so tightly her hands
were numb. The sun crossed overhead and the car's shadow
hugged its passage, then began to lengthen ahead of them.
Jeff had been dozing, she was sure, but now he began to
fidget. One hand plucked insistently at her jeans.

"I have to go potty, Mommy. And I'm hungry," he
whined.

It was past noon, she realized. Her own fear had numbed
her to physical needs, but Jeff was only a child. She glanced
at Matt.

"Can we stop?"

"No."

"But he—"

"Shut up! Don't tell me what he wants or we'll pull over
and dump him here on the side of the road!"

Jeff's face puckered uncertainly. Kay brushed her hand across his golden head in anguished consolation. If she could be certain Matt would abandon Jeff unharmed, she'd call his bluff. But he was too crafty for that. A child alone on the highway would attract immediate attention from the first car that passed. And Jeff was old enough to give a description of Matt as well as his name. If the police didn't already know Matt was in the area, they would then.

She couldn't resist watching the clock now. Minutes dragged by as the miles fell behind. They passed towns that had never been anything but names to her before. She and Elliot had never driven this far, and she had no conception of the geography of the eastern part of the state. She was driving automatically now, numbed by fatigue and fear. When she first noticed the blinking light ahead, it didn't register. When it did, she tensed. A roadblock? The police? Her tongue tasted metallic.

Matt hunched forward, squinting through the windshield. His breath hissed as he brought up his hand. The knife glinted like a feral eye.

"Slow down," he ordered.

Jeff looked up eagerly. "Are we going to stop now, Mommy?"

Matt backhanded him with a vicious blow. "Shut up, you stupid kid!"

Howling, Jeff raised a small fist to pound on Matt furiously. Matt cuffed him again and shoved him back in the seat. Jeff fell against Kay, sobbing. Her heart thundering, she put her arm around him protectively. The car veered to the edge of the road as she tried to steer with one hand.

Matt snarled, "Leave him alone. He ain't hurt. You drive real nice and careful now, you hear? Or maybe he *will* get hurt."

Swallowing her panic, Kay put both hands back on the wheel. Sniffling, Jeff drew away, as though she were no longer a source of assurance. He sensed her terror, and he knew it was greater than his.

Gradually the blinking lights formed an arrow to funnel traffic to a single lane. Orange signs and flapping flags warned of road work ahead. Kay slowed to a crawl as she saw the flagman in a bright orange vest. A heavy roller chugged noisily in the other lane, and the pungent smell of tar filled the car. Matt pulled Jeff onto his lap.

The flagman held up a slow sign and waved them through. He didn't even glance at the station wagon as it went past. Kay wanted to shout, *"Help us!"* but he was already gazing past them down the road, bored with the monotony of his job. She swallowed acid disappointment as she realized there would be no miracles. There wasn't anyone to help them. She and Jeff were completely at Matt's mercy unless *she* found a way out. She had to admit what she had tried to ignore: Matt had not found her by chance. He'd kept track of her while he was locked behind prison walls, and he'd come after her with a purpose.

Just as he had eleven years ago.

7

A dusty blanket of heat lay on the barn, making it hard to breathe. The dry air tickled Kathy's throat so she had to be very careful not to cough. Even though her father was in his workshop across the mummified yard, he'd hear and know where she was. It was as if she put out signals, like a radio, that he could tune in at will. She burrowed deeper into the stiff, sweet hay.

She hated him, even if he was her father. He sure didn't think she was so great either. Matter of fact, she was positive he hated her. Everything he did proved it. Maybe that's why it was so easy to lie here wondering what it would be like if he was dead instead of Ma. Her eyes burned and tears crawled down her cheeks as the dry spot in her throat became a dust ball. She pressed her hand over her mouth and buried her face as the cough exploded. When it passed, she lay very still, her whole body tense. Only the shrill noise of the crickets complaining about the heat broke the silence.

Not her father's saw . . . or hammering . . . She was alert instantly, listening. Had he heard her? Was he still in the workshop? She squeezed her eyes shut tight, praying.

"Come down from there, girl!"

She bolted up in astonishment. He was in the barn—right under her—and she hadn't heard a sound! She scooted

35

across the rough floorboards to the ladder. Dust swirled in the shaft of sunlight coming through the hay doors.

He was beside an empty stanchion, working the trip lock with his blunt fingers. He didn't look up, as though she didn't deserve a glance. Nervously she swung her feet and felt for the ladder. Her throat was dry and tickly again but she was too scared to cough. When she reached the apron, she stared at her father nervously until he turned. Even then he didn't look at her.

"You got work to do. Get at it."

"Yes, Pa."

"Don't let me catch you talking on the phone, hear?"

"Yes, Pa."

"That boy calls, you tell him I'll have his hide he comes round here pestering you. He ain't no good. You tell him."

She looked at her dirty tennis shoes as her neck prickled with goose bumps.

"You hear? Answer me, girl!"

"I hear, Pa."

"You need a good whippin', sassin' like that." His eyes glittered like moths close to a flame. His mouth was a thin, hard line.

"I don't mean to sass, Pa."

"Your ma'd turn over in her grave, seeing what you've grown to. Fine example you set for Tommy." He shook his head as if the end of the world was at hand. "I should have let the county take you when your ma went. A man's got no business trying to bring up a daughter by hisself."

He made it an obscene word: *daughter*. Kathy clenched her jaw to keep from crying. Why did he even pretend to care when all the time he hated her because she was alive and Ma was dead? He blamed her for Ma. She saw it every time he looked at the empty chair at the table.

Her father sighed as if his burden was too much to carry. "Get up to the house like you're told. What are you standing here for?" His calloused hand moved with lightning speed, stinging her cheek sharply. She ran, her face burning with tears.

They ate supper in silence. Afterward, Pa and Tommy sat in the living room watching TV while she did the dishes. From time to time she heard Tommy laugh. She wondered how he felt about Pa. Pa treated him better than her, but Tommy was only five. Ma had died right after . . .

She sudsed a dish and dipped it in the rinse water. If the truant officer hadn't come, Pa would have kept her home to take care of the motherless baby. He resented paying a woman to come in until Kathy got home from school. Fat Mrs. Crowley, who changed the baby's diapers and fed him. "I don't do housework, Mr. Gerrett. I'm a babysitter. You want a cleaning woman, you hire one."

Pa didn't. He had Kathy. At first, with her aching loneliness for her mother, Kathy didn't miss playing in the schoolyard or stopping off at one of her classmate's to do homework. She had grown up with chores and was used to hard work. But no girl should be robbed of her whole life. The resentment began when she got to high school. It was different then. In high school it was important to spend some time with the other kids, to be part of things. There were clubs and sports and parties. And boys.

Kathy blushed as she remembered the taunting laughter when Elise Halvetson asked her right in front of the whole lunchroom who was taking her to the spring dance. Elise, with her silky blond hair and green eyes, had boys trailing after her like bees after nectar. They all laughed because they knew no one ever asked Kathy Gerrett to go anywhere. Even if she had been allowed to go, no one would ask her.

Except someday it would be different. Someone would ask her, and she'd dance and laugh and—She plunged her hands into the soapy water. Who'd ever ask her? No one, that's who. The only boy who ever talked to her was Matt Briggs, and he was too old for kid stuff like high school hops. If only he hadn't called on the phone last night, her father would never know she had a friend, even though they hardly knew each other. Matt Briggs was an outcast, a loner. You couldn't live in Blue Canyon and not hear plenty about Matt Briggs. His father was no-account and his mother drank. Matt had been in trouble since the time he could walk, getting into other people's things and fighting when kids called him names. By the time he was sixteen he'd been expelled from school so many times, no one was surprised he dropped out. After that he did odd jobs here and there when he could get them or until he screwed up and got fired.

The past few weeks he'd been driving the delivery truck for Rasmun's Feed Store. He stopped to talk to her several times, always far enough from the house so her father didn't see. Yesterday she'd told Matt about the calico having kittens, and that her father wanted to get rid of them because there were too many cats around the barn. Last night Matt called. Pa handed her the phone, then stood where he could hear every word. Afterward she wanted to pretend it was someone from school asking about homework, but her father would have known she was lying. So she told him Matt Briggs had found a home for the kittens.

Her father was more interested in how she knew Matt Briggs. She mixed a lie with a bit of truth and said Matt had asked directions while he was trying to return a lost cat he'd found on the road. She hadn't meant any harm telling him about the calico's litter.

This morning, when she went out to feed the chickens, the kittens were a sodden dead heap beside the water trough.

She swished her hands in the dishwater in search of the silverware. The tip of a sharp knife caught her, and she pulled out her hand with a gasp. Bright blood oozed across her thumb. Using her other hand, she found a tissue in her jeans pocket to wrap around the cut. Cautiously, she felt in the sink for the carving knife, rinsed it, and laid it on the edge of the drain. She was letting the water out of the sink when she heard a soft tap at the back door. Matt Briggs beckoned to her from the shadows of the porch. Startled, she glanced toward the sound of the television. Eyes wide, she motioned him to go away. He gestured insistently until she opened the door and slipped out into the darkness.

"Pa will kill you! You'd better go before he hears us."

"I ain't afraid of your pa."

"Please—"

She'd waited for him on the road this afternoon to tell him about the kittens and warn him not to call again. She hadn't been able to hold back the tears as she told him about the piles of wet fur that had been five tiny, mewling lives. Matt looked at her for a long time, then climbed down from the truck and put his arms around her and told her not to cry. She pulled away, terrified that someone would see them and tell her father. Matt didn't try to hold her again, but he touched her hair gently and said everything would be all right.

But it wasn't. Matt was here on the back porch with Pa only a few yards away in the living room. Suppose he turned off the TV? Or came out to the kitchen for a bottle of beer? She was sure her heart had stopped beating.

"Please, Matt. It will just cause trouble. My pa isn't feeling good and he's cranky."

"He's always cranky. He's a bastard, that's what he is," Matt said in a tight voice. "He's a bastard for killing those kittens and making you cry."

It was like being dropped into an icy pool to hear her own evil thoughts put in plain language. She glanced apprehensively through the window. Had something moved in the hall?

She reached for the doorknob. "I'll see you tomorrow on the road. After school."

"I came to take you for a ride. I got the truck down on the road."

"I can't."

"Sure you can. Your pa won't mind you going out for a few minutes, what with him feeling so lousy and all. You got the dishes done. I saw you."

He'd been watching her. How long had he been out here in the dark? She should go in. She was making things worse standing here, but she kept remembering how warm his arms had been around her and how gently he'd touched her hair.

Matt said, "I'll talk to your pa. I'll ask him if it's okay for us to go for a ride."

"No—don't do that." Her stomach lurched the way it did when her father drove the pickup over the double dips near the gas station on the county road.

"I'm going to, Katie, no matter what you say. Now you go on down and wait in the van. Me and your pa'll talk man to man." When she didn't move, he brushed his hand across the damp sweat cooling on her forehead, pushing back a wisp of hair that had fallen in her eyes. "Go on, Katie. If he says no, I'll never bother you again, I promise. Go wait in the van."

She moved in a daze, putting one foot in front of the other down the long slope of the lane, climbing into the van and leaving the door ajar because she was afraid to slam it. Pa would never say yes, not in a million years. She shouldn't have let Matt go in. Pa would take out his anger on her. But suppose, just suppose, Matt talked him into it?

She strained in the darkness, listening to the night crickets. Once she thought she heard loud voices from the house, but with the breeze rustling the elms at the foot of the lane, she couldn't be sure. When she finally saw a figure coming down the lane, she blinked. It was Matt. His windbreaker was zipped to the neck and his hands were jammed in his pockets. She held her breath as he opened the door and climbed behind the wheel. A pale splash of moonlight through the windshield made deep shadows on his face. His teeth were clenched and his eyes were hidden under his tightly drawn brows. He sucked air into his lungs as if he were coming up from a deep dive. Finally he looked at her.

"He said it's okay."

She gaped at him. Immediately, she began to doubt. "He did? You're sure? He said I could go?"

Matt stabbed the key in the ignition. "That's what he said, okay. You don't hear him calling you back, do you?"

She realized that was exactly what her father would do if he'd refused Matt's request. He'd be standing out on the porch yelling for her so the whole county could hear. So he must have said yes. She was so excited she couldn't think straight.

The engine turned and caught. Matt let out the clutch too fast, and the van jerked forward, spitting gravel. The door beside Kathy swung open and she dived for it. Matt grabbed her arm so she didn't tumble out. She slammed the door and sat back, smiling when Matt didn't let go of her hand.

They drove up toward Beech Creek Summit. When Matt parked the van in a deserted picnic area, they walked to the edge of the creek where a still pool glittered in the moonlight. For the first time since her mother died, she felt close to another human being. It wasn't just the physical touch of her hand and Matt's, but something deep inside. She felt understood. Free. Matt talked about little things, like hating to have to tell the people who promised to take the kittens they were gone, and how hard he worked for Mr. Rasmun at the feed store, and how someday he was going to have a business of his own, with no one telling him what to do. He was easy to listen to, and she was happy being with him until conscience began to warp her pleasure. It was getting late. She told Matt she had to go back. Her father would have a fit if she stayed out much later.

Matt picked up a flat stone and cocked his arm like a pitcher. The rock skimmed across the moonlit pool.

."Five skips. Did you see that?" He grinned proudly. Then his face sobered and he put his hands on her shoulders. "Katie, you don't have to go back."

"Are you kidding? Pa would kill me if I stayed out all night."

"No, I mean it, you're not going back. I won't let you."

She laughed nervously, cold suddenly. "I have to. My pa—

"Your pa doesn't want you."

She swallowed hard with the feeling of her own evil thoughts coming to life again.

"We had a long talk, me and your pa. I gotta admit at first he didn't want you to go with me."

She had heard yelling. . . .

"He was all for going down to the van and dragging you back so he could beat the shit outta you." When she started to shake, his hands tightened on her shoulders. "I told him I love you, and I got the right to court you proper. If'n you don't want me, that's for you to decide, not him."

She stared at him. His eyes were dark pits in the pale mask of his face. She felt the pressure of each of his ten fingers on her flesh. No one had spoken the word "love" to her for a very long time.

"I tried to make him listen to reason, but your pa's a stubborn old fool. I guess you know that, don't you?" He was watching her. She stood very still, not sure if she should answer. Matt cocked his head and pulled her closer. He smelled of bay rum, the way her father did when he went to the bank or the bowling alley. "Katie, your pa don't want you to come home. He said if you went with me you'd better not come back. He said—he said you ain't his daughter no more."

She stood paralyzed. The emotions she hadn't been able to untangle all evening now were a suffocating net. She struggled for breath. Matt's hands were like talons on her shoulders. Then she was sobbing and crying, and Matt was rocking her in his arms.

8

"Why do I have the feeling you're holding out on me, Harriet?" Ed Viemont dropped ice cubes into a glass and poured scotch over them. The steaks were sizzling on the grill, sending up a tantalizing aroma.

"What would I hold out? Kay is missing and—"

"Kay is *gone* from the cabin. That's a little different, Harriet." He watched her, trying to read the expression on her face. He was sure she hadn't told him everything. It had to be the Pier woman's past that Harriet felt would be a violation of trust to reveal. After their phone conversation, he'd rummaged in the back files at the *Press* office to find issues covering the time of Briggs's original rampage, capture, and trial. There'd been a girl with him. A girl who'd now be a woman. Studying the faded photos of Kathy Gerrett, he tried to picture the face eleven years later.

He settled his squat, muscular body into the chair and lifted his boots to the porch rail. Moths flitted at the bug lights as curling plumes of smoke from the barbecue drifted into the night. Harriet was quiet.

"Newspapermen print the news, but there's no law says they can't speculate in private."

She looked at him. "Meaning?"

"We've known each other a long time. I've learned to read your signs."

She laughed. "Like bear spoor?"

"Something like that." He grinned. "I get here a half hour early, but I don't find you rushing around doing last-minute stuff. I find you standing on the front steps waiting for me. Not that I'm complaining, mind you. I like a woman who can tell time." He patted her hand and winked. "Not only are you waiting for me, you've got the fire going, the potatoes baking, the salad made, and a fresh apple pie cooling. Mighty efficient. These are the signs I read, Harriet. Signs of a restless afternoon. You couldn't sit still. You never can when you've got a problem on your mind. Wayne used to say it kept him from starving to death, the way you cooked up a storm when you were worried."

She stared into the dark ring of woods surrounding the cabin and didn't answer.

"Want to know what I think?"

She nodded without turning.

"Kay Pier was once Kathy Gerrett, and you think she may have something to worry about now that Matt Briggs has escaped." He heard Harriet's softly indrawn breath.

"How do you figure that?" she asked, not confirming, not denying.

"You ask if there's any news on the escape. You're worried about your neighbor, whose name happens to be Kay, maybe for Kathryn, Kathy. A coincidence or a connection? I spent a few hours with my old files. She's changed a lot. I don't think I would have recognized her without the thought being planted in my mind."

Harriet looked at him, asking for compassion. "She's suffered so much already, Ed. It's taken her a long time to get over the past. She's paid her debt a hundred times over."

"You think she was innocent like she claimed?"

"It happens I do. Oh, I don't say she was totally without guilt, but she was a scared, mixed-up kid. She went along with Briggs for the wrong reasons and stayed with him as

long as she did for even crazier ones, but I don't think she
knew he butchered her father and brother.''

"What about the slaughter of innocents along the way?"

Harriet sighed. "You can blind yourself to a lot of things
if you're riddled with guilt."

Interested, he asked, "What'd she have to be guilty
about?"

"Leaving home. Her father was a tyrant. She wanted to
run away, but she clung to the only family she had. She
needed to be loved."

Ed got up and used the long-handled tongs to turn the
meat. Fat sizzled on the coals. He checked Harriet's drink,
but she waved him off.

"That issue's not at stake here," she said. "Whatever
her guilt or fear was, discovering Matt Briggs has escaped
has to be a terrible trauma for her right now." She gazed
at him across the soft gloom.

Ed cocked his head. "I get the feeling again you're holding back."

"Why?"

"You said 'discovered,' not 'heard.' "

"I guess I did."

Ed's iron-gray brows drew together as he studied her.
"If you've got any suspicions, Harriet, you'd better tell
me. Briggs is dangerous."

She drew a deep breath. "I went back up to the cabin
after I talked to you. There's still no sign of them but—"

"But what?" he prodded.

"I walked around the clearing a dozen times. It's not
like those damned TV shows where I found a matchbook
from Soledad or a button from Briggs's prison shirt. But I
felt a presence, sort of a lingering scent of danger, as if
he'd been there and imprinted the nest."

"Did you find anything?"

She looked at him, but he couldn't read her gaze. Finally
she said, "A spot where the grass was trampled as though
someone slid down the hill in back."

"The kid."

"The mess Kay left behind."

"Everyone is careless once in a while."

She shook her head. "I've been telling myself these same things all afternoon, but I can't shake off the feeling I have down here." She tapped her abdomen. "I'm worried. I want everything to be just what you're saying and have Kay and Jeff turn up safe and sound in Los Angeles. But suppose Briggs *was* there? Suppose he's got her now? By the time we're sure she's not safe in L.A., they could be three states away."

Ed laid the turning fork on the tray of the Weber. Behind him, a wreath of pale smoke lifted into the September darkness. He walked slowly back to his chair. "Have you tried calling her?"

"There's no answer, but she could still be on the road." She'd placed another call to New York as well, only to learn from Trevor that Elliot was already en route home.

Ed was silent a few moments, lost in thought. When at last he looked at her, his dark eyes were questioning. "Do you think we should call the sheriff?"

She sucked air into her lungs and held it as though it would ease her pain. "I haven't been able to figure out anything we can do without the law. But if I'm wrong—" She shook her head and pressed her fingertips to her temple. "The media will have a field day. I don't want to put Kay through that again."

"There's something that doesn't seem to have occurred to you." Ed met her inquiring look squarely. "The police may get the notion that Kay Pier went with Briggs of her own accord."

"She would never—"

He raised a blunt-fingered hand. "You believe that, but they may not. She went with him once before. There's a good chance some people are going to think she did it again."

Harriet shut her eyes and clamped her lips to a tight line of denial.

"Now, do you think we should call the sheriff without talking to Elliot first?" Ed asked softly.

9

Elliot shoved a twenty at the driver and had the double locks on the front door undone before the cab pulled away. The house was dark, the quiet kind of dark that comes with emptiness. He stalked through the rooms snapping on lights and leaving a blazing trail.

"Kay? Jeff?"

The gold and white living room and dining room overlooking the canyon were empty, the kitchen pristine. In the soft blue bedroom the king-size bed hadn't been slept in; there was no sign of suitcases. Still, he checked Jeff's room and the glass-walled den overlooking the patio. When there was no place left to look, he sank onto a stool at the kitchen bar, his hand on the phone.

He'd worked enough police beats to know the cops wouldn't lift a pen to a missing person report on someone who'd been gone only a few hours. There were plenty of reasons Kay might not be home yet. She got a late start. Car trouble. She decided to stay overnight in a motel because Jeff was giving her a hard time. Jeez, he'd nagged her to do it if she got tired. Maybe this time she had. And she wouldn't even try to get in touch. He was supposed to be in New York, not here worrying his guts into knots.

He glanced at the clock. It was an ungodly hour, but he dialed Harriet's number.

"I'm in L.A., Harriet. Is Kay there? Have you heard from her?"

"I've been trying to call you. No, she isn't. Ed Viemont is here. We think we should call the sheriff, but we didn't want to do it without talking to you."

The coffee he'd consumed during the flight congealed in his stomach. "What's happened?"

Quickly, Harriet described the disarray at the cabin and her concern over Kay's hasty departure. "Ed's in touch with the highway patrol," she said. "We just heard they think Briggs could be headed this way."

He didn't recognize his voice. "Why?"

She told him about the stolen trucks, and the most recent news that the pickup from Coalinga had been found disabled on a secondary road near Yuba City. No trail had been picked up from there.

Yuba City was less than a hundred miles from the cabin. Elliot slumped against the counter, fighting nausea.

"Elliot?"

"Thanks, Harriet. I'll be there as soon as I can."

"Wait until morning, Elliot. The seven o'clock plane will get you here faster than you can drive. I'll pick you up at the airport." She hesitated. "What about the sheriff?"

He shivered as though a cold wind had swept the stuffy room. "Call him."

"Elliot?"

"Yeah?"

"Get some rest. Tomorrow may be a long day."

Double jet lag had his head pounding. He swallowed three aspirin and stretched out on the sofa, letting his mind float in limbo, creating nightmare visions about the danger Kay and Jeff might be in. At four, he went back to the kitchen and dialed the *Times*.

"You're supposed to be on vacation. Printing ink in your veins or some such shit?" Wagner Jones sounded glad of the interruption.

"Something like that." Elliot was relieved that Jones

answered the phone. He was new and didn't know about Kay's past. "Will you do me a favor, Wag?"

"Name it, noble brother of the Fourth Estate."

"What's the morning edition got on the Matt Briggs escape from Soledad?"

"Front-page stuff, m'lad. Want me to read it to you?"

"A quick summary."

Jones sighed. "They discovered he was gone Thursday about noon. One of those official foul-ups where everyone figured someone else had him, and he took off while they were arguing about it. Stole a laundry truck from a joint where there were a dozen parked during lunch hour. He had almost two hours' head start before they were even looking for him. Next heard from again in Coalinga. A pickup this time. It wasn't reported missing until yesterday. Found nine o'clock last night near Yuba City. Whereabouts of fugitive unknown. Considered dangerous, may be armed, may be disguised, you name it. Every highway patrol station has his mug shot and a copy of his prints. Dragnet. Tum-de-dum-dum."

Elliot was cold. "Are we recapping his original crimes?"

"You'd better believe it, Bucko. Mad Dog Matt rides again. From what I hear, we were the ones who tagged him with the nickname. He's going to have a resurrection second only to J.C. himself."

Elliot fought for control. "How many 'graphs did the rehash get?"

"Four, all dripping with blood."

"Any mention of the girl?"

"Hit and run: 'Briggs's companion on his murder spree, Kathy Gerrett, served five years in the Women's Correctional Institution at Frontera and was released in 1979.' "

Sweat beaded at Elliot's temples. "Any pictures?"

"A charming one of Mad Dog looking vicious when he was taken into custody."

None of Kay, thank God.

"Thanks, Wag."

"You on to something, Bucko? I could use a little scoop to shake the minions."

"Just curious. See you next week." He hung up before Wagner could ask questions.

10

Matt told her to turn off the interstate a few miles past Elko. He pulled a worn, folded map from his pocket, studied it intently, then directed her onto a county road that cut across the desolate landscape of the northeastern corner of the state. The growing realization that Matt knew where they were headed terrified Kay. She tried to visualize a map but couldn't summon the most rudimentary geography to mind. California, Nevada—the end of the world. Not Oregon . . . not Blue Canyon—*Elliot, Elliot, help me!*

She'd given up hope of signaling a passing car. Even when Matt seemed to be staring out the window, she knew he was watching her. The knife, hidden beside the door, was a constant threat. And since they'd left the interstate there hadn't been half a dozen other cars on the road. Occasionally they rode through a tiny town where the dust settled behind them without notice. At one that was no more than some scattered buildings at a crossroad, Matt ordered her to turn in at a shabby gas station. He roused Jeff from his dozing lethargy and held him on his lap while a pimplefaced youth filled the tank and took the money Matt shoved at him. They were under way in minutes. A half hour later, on an empty stretch of the two-lane blacktop, he told her to stop so Jeff could "go potty." When he said she could get out too, she was terrified Matt might drive off with Jeff.

Kay lost track of time and distance. When she glanced

at the odometer, she couldn't remember what it had read before. She could no longer ignore her growing hunger as Jeff began to squirm restlessly. He'd had only a bowl of cereal before they set out for the airport. Hours ago. A lifetime ago. An eternity ago. She was so thirsty her tongue felt bruised, but when she glanced at Matt, he was absorbed in his own thoughts, a hint of a smile touching the corners of his mouth. He seemed calm, but he was like a cat that could spring without warning. Watching the road from under heavy-lidded eyes, he seemed close to sleep. When he spoke suddenly, she gave a start.

"Turn here."

She braked, almost missing the narrow overgrown trail. She hesitated.

"Turn!" Matt raised the knife like an arrow. Jeff cringed and edged closer to Kay.

As she steered onto the rutted path, the tires bounced in potholes carved by long-forgotten rains and gravel spat at the undercarriage. A pasture? Open range? She scanned the hillside for cattle but saw only scraggly sagebrush and wild grass. Her momentary inattention made the car veer and scrape some bushes.

"Watch what you're doing!" Matt banged the flat of the knife against the dash.

Jeff jumped and buried his face against his mother. Kay bit her lip. She had to keep control. She had to—

"Stop!" Matt ordered.

She hit the brake, thrusting out her arm to keep Jeff from pitching forward. *Seat belts . . . I should have fastened them,* she thought. No, they'd make it harder to run if the chance came.

Matt opened the door and stepped out into the molten sunshine. He shielded his eyes as he looked around. Unconsciously, Kay's foot eased on the brake. She hadn't shifted into park, and the car crept forward. The faint motion made her react instinctively. She slammed the accelerator. The Olds leaped. The swinging door cracked Matt, spinning him back.

Kay gripped the wheel as she struggled to control the bucking car jouncing across the washboard furrows. In the rear-view mirror, a cloud of dust enveloped Matt.

"Mommy!" Jeff clung to her.

"Hang on, Jeff, hang on!"

The car careered as the tires sank into ruts, spun out. Suddenly the trail angled sharply. Kay fought the wheel as the undercarriage dragged. Then, without warning, the path ended at a riverbank. She hit the brake desperately as the car nosed toward the rocky riverbed where a sluggish trickle of water remained after the summer drought. The rear wheels caught at the last moment and the car shuddered to a stop.

Sobbing, Kay slammed the gear lever into reverse. The Olds rocked, faltered, then finally dug its way backward up the slope. Frantically, she looked for a place to turn, but walls of gray-green sage hugged the car. Sobbing, she glanced at the mirror and saw Matt appear out of the settling dust like an apparition, his long strides chopping off the distance between them. She hit the gas pedal savagely. The car raced back. *She'd kill him. She'd drive over him a thousand times until he was ground into the dust and—*

The door flew open. Running and cursing as he tried to keep up, Matt grabbed Jeff.

"Mommy! Mommy!" Jeff's scream was a terrified wail as Matt yanked him from the car.

"Oh, God! Jeffffff—" Kay slammed the brake. The engine stalled. She jumped out as the car jerked to a stop. "Jeff!" She ran toward them.

Matt slammed Jeff against the hood of the car and put the butcher knife to his throat. Jeff's eyes glazed with terror.

Kay stopped, her pulse thundering. Matt didn't look up from the poised knife. "Matt," she said shakily. "I'm sorry. I didn't know what I was doing. I thought—I don't know what I thought—''

He flicked her a glance. "Bitch!" Looking back at Jeff, he applied enough pressure to make a thin red welt as he drew the knife across Jeff's throat.

Kay stifled a cry as Jeff's face went white. Her voice was a whisper. "I'm really sorry, Matt. Please don't be mad. Don't hurt him. I won't make any more trouble. Don't hurt him."

Matt's breath hissed as he looked up. She forced herself to meet his gaze though she was shaking so badly it was hard to breathe.

Finally Matt said, "Okay. But remember, Katie, I don't need no stupid kid fuckin' things up, you know?"

She nodded. "I won't make any trouble."

"You promise?"

Her bones turned to ice. "I promise."

He let go of Jeff, who collapsed to his hands and knees, whimpering. Kay riveted her gaze on Matt until he slipped the knife into his belt.

"Get the sandwiches."

She got the cooler from the back of the car. Matt gestured impatiently. She balanced the cooler on one hip and bent to help Jeff up. He clung to her leg, crying pitifully. She patted his bowed head, then took his hand and followed Matt down the bank. Matt sat on a smooth rock beside a shallow pool of water. Kay found a flat spot a few feet away where there was room for Jeff beside her. He was rubbing his throat in hurt silence and refused to look at her.

How had Matt known the river was here? And that there was no way out except the single trail? He'd been certain of the path and known she couldn't escape. Matt astonished her by producing paper cups that she recognized from her own cupboard. She didn't remember his taking them. Was she losing her mind? He passed them for her to fill with the tepid orange juice. He gulped his and held out the cup for a refill as he picked up a sandwich.

They ate in silence, washing away their thirst with water from the stream when the juice was gone. Jeff chewed like a programmed robot. When she held the cup to his lips, he swallowed obediently without looking up.

Matt wiped his mouth with the back of his hand. "Let's go." He crunched up the paper cup and tossed it into the grass.

Kay picked up the cooler. When she reached for Jeff's hand, he pulled away. She struggled against the tears stinging her eyes. Remembering the heat of the car and Jeff's thirst, she glanced at the feeble flow of the river.

"There's a plastic bottle in the back of the car," she said tentatively. "We could take some water with us."

Matt hesitated, then nodded. He motioned her toward the car and fell in step behind her, leaving Jeff to trail behind. Kay fumbled with the trunk lock under Matt's watchful eye. When she got the tailgate open and lifted the well cover, the tire iron atop the spare glowed like a lighthouse beacon. Her hand hesitated, but before her brain could weigh the odds Matt scooped Jeff into the tight circle of his arm again and smiled tauntingly. Quickly she pushed aside the iron and dug in the corner for the plastic container.

"Get the water," Matt ordered. He made no move to put Jeff down or follow her as she ran back toward the river.

She had to pick her way among the wet rocks to find a pool deep enough to submerge the mouth of the bottle. In her haste, she stirred up mud so the water turned milky and she had to find another pool. Water sloshed on her jeans and shoes, but she didn't notice. When the container was half full she capped it and ran back. Matt was behind the wheel, Jeff strapped beside him.

"Put it in back. You sit up here."

As soon as she slammed the door, Matt backed up until

he found a spot wide enough to turn. He drove inexpertly, jerking from reverse to drive so the car bucked. When they got back to the county road, the tires screeched as the Olds wheeled onto the blacktop.

Jeff hadn't made a sound since Matt put the knife to his throat. He was deathly pale under his summer tan, and his face was streaked with grime and tears. She longed to comfort him but didn't dare set Matt off again. Finally, when Jeff's head lolled, she drew him down into her lap and felt his brow. It was cool and dry. Was that a symptom of shock? She tried to remember the baby books she'd studied so diligently during Jeff's early years, but the pages of her memory were blank.

The sun lingered behind the hills before it sank beyond the invisible horizon, taking the last of the twilight with it. Matt turned on the headlights. She was thankful for his silence now. She'd been a fool to pull that dumb stunt at the river. She'd ignored all the warning signs that should have told her Matt knew what lay ahead at every turn. He'd frightened Jeff badly and it had all been for naught. She'd only made matters worse.

She was tired and cold. She'd had the presence of mind to pick up Jeff's sweater as they left the cabin, but she was wearing only a short-sleeved blouse.

"Can I get Jeff's sweater?" she asked.

Matt glanced around as though he'd forgotten he wasn't alone. He looked at the sleeping child and nodded. Kay found the sweater and spread it over Jeff without waking him. In the dim light, she saw the dark circles beneath his eyes, the pallor of his skin. A lump formed under her breastbone. *He's so young and innocent . . . none of this is his fault. . . .* Drained, she lay her head back and closed her eyes, trying to ignore the seeping cold. They had crossed into Idaho. She'd seen the change in highway signs. Mentally she tried to catalogue all the cities and towns she knew in Idaho, but her befuddled brain balked. She slid over the edge of sleep abruptly.

When she came to groggily, the car had slowed. They were on the outskirts of a town. The street was dark except for a few isolated house lights. What time was it? As the car crossed an intersection, she saw a well-lighted avenue two blocks away. She stayed very still so Matt wouldn't know she was awake as she squinted in the darkness for signs. It seemed important to know where they were.

At the corner, Matt turned away from the lights. Tears stung Kay's eyes, and she blinked them away angrily. She couldn't whine and snivel every time her hopes were dashed, she lectured herself. Jeff's life depended on her. His weight on her lap was reassuring.

She frowned as she realized they'd made another right turn, then another. Matt was going around the block. Small, shabby houses stood behind dark yards and deserted sidewalks. On one corner, a mom and pop grocery store was etched in the faint glow of a night light. Opposite it, a boarded-up filling station with derelict gas pumps crouched in shadows. Matt pulled in, stopped, then reversed until the car was between the building and a high hedge. He shut off the ignition. Kay held her breath.

Matt slid soundlessly from behind the wheel, outlined momentarily in the dim glow of the overhead light. Kay followed his movements as he came around the car. When she saw the butcher knife in his hand, she leaned over Jeff protectively, trying to summon her wits and energy from the foggy depths of sleep. It took a moment to realize Matt was hunched in the station doorway. A moment later she heard the knife scraping wood as he worked at the hasp. Wood splintered, and Matt shouldered the door open. He came back to the car.

"Be quiet and he won't get hurt," he warned in a low tone as he pulled her out. She tried to hold on to Jeff, but Matt yanked her away from the car and shoved her through the dark doorway. Her hands met cold stone as she pitched forward into the black void. Behind her, Matt crouched in the doorway.

"The kid's going with me, so don't try anything, you hear? If I come back and there's anyone around or you ain't here, he gets it."

Terror strangled her. "Don't hurt him!" she begged.

"Do what I say and he stays in one piece. It's up to you."

She nodded, then, realizing he couldn't see her, whispered desperately, "Yes . . . yes. Just don't hurt him. I'll do whatever you say." She crawled in supplication, oblivious to the concrete scraping her knees. Matt shoved her away.

"I'll be back. You wait."

"Please—"

"Promise!"

Fighting hysteria, she pressed her hands to her face. "I promise—I promise!"

Matt rose, a silent shadow, and the door began to close.

"Matt!" The door stopped. "Promise you won't hurt him if I wait. *Promise! Say it!*"

The door shut with a thump. She threw herself at it but Matt braced it tightly as he fastened the hasp. Kay raised her fists to pound but caught herself just in time. *No noise. No trouble.* She pressed her face to the rotting wood, listening. Was it her imagination or had she heard Matt's voice? Tears overflowed as she heard the car drive away.

I did hear him, she told herself. *I heard him. He promised.*

11

Kay huddled in the darkness. The walls were squeezing in. *Count from one to a hundred—Say the alphabet backward—Sing . . . "When the saints go marching in—"*

Pray . . . "Now I lay me down to sleep, I pray the Lord my soul to keep; if I should die before I wake—"

Matt wouldn't hurt Jeff. He promised. She heard him. She had, she *had!*

Shivering, she forced herself to stir. Hands out like a blind man, she groped her way around the tiny room. It was no more than four by four feet. Smaller than a prison cell. A washroom. The faint stench of urine clung in the air. The sink had been ripped out, leaving capped pipes. The seatless toilet was a broken hulk.

She retreated to a corner near the door and sank to the floor. Hugging her knees, she rested her head. Jeff's terrified face was a haunting accusation. *Let him sleep quietly.* If he woke and found her gone, he'd panic. Crying upset Matt. He used to—

She pushed the thought away desperately. If she began to relive the past, she'd go crazy. Think about now. *Jeff, I love you. Be a good boy. Don't do anything to upset Matt.* If only she hadn't fallen asleep, she'd know where they were, what town this was. Where was Matt headed? Did she want to know? She felt helpless as guilt gathered like a dust devil.

She could no longer tell hours from minutes. Now and

then she raised her head at some sound, real or imagined, but the world ceased to exist except for the black nightmare of the cell.

When she became aware of a soft scrabbling noise, it took several moments to realize someone was at the door. When it opened, she cringed in the blinding beam of a flashlight. Behind it, Matt's face was a featureless skull. As he pulled her to her feet, her legs buckled with needles of pain. He grabbed her and led her outside.

She hadn't heard the car . . .

"I came back, Katie."

He was holding her so close, she smelled his stale sweat. She tried to pull away as terror brought her back to life.

"Where's Jeff?"

Matt stiffened. "I came back like I promised," he repeated angrily.

Kay forced down her hysteria. "I'm glad, Matt. I kept my promise too. I didn't yell or try to get out. I kept my promise, I did—Oh, God—*where's Jeff?*" A tiny mewling sound escaped her lips as she searched the street for the bulky outline of the Oldsmobile.

Matt yanked her past the hedge to a small car at the curb. Opening the door, he shoved her in. She glimpsed a dark bundle on the back seat and twisted to touch it. When Jeff whimpered sleepily, she collapsed and buried her face in her hands.

Matt got behind the wheel and started the engine. She tried to control her sobs. Jeff was safe. Matt hadn't hurt him. When she finally looked up, Matt's face was a shadow carved in the darkness, but she could see the hard set of his jaw. He was angry because she'd asked about Jeff.

She wet her lips. "Thank you, Matt," she finally managed to say. His tension didn't ease. She pushed away memories that wanted to crack through the wall of the past. "I knew you'd keep your promise, Matt. I knew you wouldn't hurt him, not after you promised." She kept talking, trying to make him forget his anger. "I really appreciate that, Matt."

She saw his shoulders relax as though an invisible wire had slipped loose. He was back from the brink. She had to be careful not to push him that far again. Whatever she did, she had to keep him calm.

Had he gotten rid of the station wagon because he was afraid it would be recognized? Were they being pursued? Or was it because the Olds was nearly out of gas again? She glanced at the dash of the strange car. Even though she couldn't make out the dials, she knew the tank was full.

Rural night enveloped them as they left the town. There were only occasional lights to mark farms set back from the road. She didn't ask where they were. It didn't matter.

Matt began to hum softly and gave Kay a sly look. "There's a present for you on the seat," he said.

She found the soft bundle. As though reading Braille, she examined the woolly sweater. She'd forgotten how cold she was. She pulled it on. She wouldn't think about where it had come from.

"Thank you, Matt." Her voice cracked.

"It's red. That's your favorite color, isn't it?"

A tight lump clogged her throat as the blood pounded in her temples. She forced herself to whisper the lie.

"Yes, I love it."

12

The sounds of morning woke her slowly. It took several minutes to recognize the noise of running water. Not a sink or toilet flushing as her father got ready for the day. Water running over rocks.

She opened her eyes and stared at the gray box over her. Sometimes she dreamed of being dead, or worse, buried alive. Had it happened? She moved cautiously and tried to sit up, but something heavy held her. She turned her head. Matt was sleeping beside her, his arm flung across her waist. She stared at the roof of the van and remembered.

Her father didn't want her anymore. Pain crowded her chest, but she refused to cry. If that was what he wanted, it would have to be. Hadn't she known all along that he hated her, no matter what he pretended?

And Matt loved her. He'd said so. He said he was courting her. She turned to look at him again. He'd held her last night while she cried until there weren't any more tears. Then he brushed the dampness from her cheeks and told her he was going to make sure she never cried again. She'd been touched by his promise, by having someone care.

They'd driven a while longer after that, slow and wandering as if they had all the time in the world. Had she asked where they were going? She didn't remember. It didn't matter, she guessed. When they finally parked in a deserted camping area, they crawled in back where Matt unfolded a blanket and pillow. He kissed her gently and held her in his arms until she fell asleep.

He looked young with his red hair plastered against his forehead and his mouth open as he breathed softly. Tommy slept like that. She'd miss him. She really didn't mind taking care of him. He was a sweet, lovable child. Who'd take care of him now?

She felt the heat of the sun on the van as she listened to the babbling stream outside. Gently, she lifted Matt's arm and slid from under it. She crawled up front and looked out the window. She couldn't see the stream but it sounded close. Quietly, she opened the door and got out.

The crisp air made her shiver. She hugged her bare arms as she realized she had nothing but the clothes on her back. What a bummer. Nothing—no purse, no comb, no change of underwear. Her cheeks warmed when she remembered she didn't have any Tampax and she'd be getting her period any day. She wondered if her father would let her get some of her things if they went back.

She walked around the van to look down at the stream. Slashes of sunlight danced on the water dropping over a rocky ledge. A few yards downstream, the bank curved sharply to form a crescent that hugged a quiet pool. Kathy inched her way down. On a small, flat spit she stepped behind a clump of bushes to relieve herself, then with a glance at the van undressed and spread her clothes over a willow. She wrapped her arms across her breasts as her nipples swelled.

Her body stiffened with the shock of the cold as she stepped into the pool. Not giving herself time to think, she plunged under and began rubbing herself briskly. When she felt clean, she started to climb out but skidded on a mossy rock and went sprawling. For a moment she was too stunned to move. Then she began to giggle as she realized her backside was sticking up in the air. Still giggling, she crawled up the slippery rock and flung herself on the grass.

It had already absorbed the sun's warmth and was like velvet. She rolled onto her back and flung out her arms, welcoming the golden sunshine. She was free. Free.

"Hey!"

She scrambled up, trying to cover her nakedness as she raced for the willows. Matt was at the edge of the bank, watching her. Kathy began to dress quickly as he started down. She pulled on her panties, then turned her back as she tugged her bra in place and fumbled with the hook.

"You got up early." He was on the other side of the bush. She reached for her T-shirt and put it on without looking at him.

"The water cold?"

She nodded. "It's freezing! I feel like an icicle."

He grinned. "Better than nuthin' though, huh? Guess I'd better take the plunge. We should start out clean. A new life and all, you know?" His gray eyes questioned her.

"Sure," she said. "Start out clean. A new life."

He sat down and began to peel off his shoes and socks. She hurried up the bank when he unsnapped his jeans. She'd never seen a man undressed. Tommy, but he was just a baby.

At the van, she opened the doors wide to air it. Then on her knees she began to straighten up. She folded the blanket, making a face when she saw the moth holes and a ragged tear across one corner. The pillow was from an old sofa; the stuffing was poking through the worn covering in half a dozen spots. She laid it on top of the blanket. Behind the driver's seat there were a pair of hiking boots with knotted laces, two pair of jeans and a paper bag stuffed with T-shirts, shorts, and socks. Crammed under the seat was an athletic bag. She pulled it out and unzipped it.

"What are you doing?" Matt scrambled up behind her and snatched the bag. He yanked the zipper closed.

"I—I was just cleaning up. I was going to put your clothes in it—" His eyes were as dark and cold as the rocks in the stream. She looked away uncomfortably, examining her fingernails and tugging at a barb of cuticle.

Matt shoved the bag under the seat and sat back on his heels. The twitch in his jaw relaxed as he looked at the neat stack of bedding.

"It looks real nice. Like a home, you know?" he said, smiling.

"I'm sorry about the bag." She didn't know what else to say.

"That's okay, but leave it alone, huh? I don't like—" He rubbed the corner of his mouth with his thumb. "A guy's gotta have something that's just his, no one else's, you know? Private. Secret." He watched her.

"Sure, Matt."

He took her hand. "You and me, we're alike, you know? Tell you what, first town we come to, I'm going to buy you a bag so you can have a secret. What's your favorite color? Red? You like red?"

She smiled ruefully. "I don't have anything to put in a bag."

Scowling, he cocked his head. "I forgot. You don't have nuthin', do you?" When she shrugged, he said, "I'll buy you stuff. Start thinking what you want. Come on—" He climbed out, pulling her along. He closed the doors, then helped her into the cab before he got behind the wheel. He started the cold engine on the third try, then slammed it in gear so fast the wheels spun. They finally caught and the van jounced uphill.

"Where are we?" Kathy asked.

He shrugged. "Gone from nowhere, goin' somewhere." He grinned and made faces until she giggled. "Right?"

"Right!"

From the highway markers, she realized they'd crossed into Idaho during the night. It felt strange being so far from home. She'd never been more than forty miles before last night. The sun streamed through the window beside her. She wondered if Pa had fed the chickens. With her gone, he'd have to do her chores as well as his own, or hire help. How was he going to like that? Maybe he'd beg her to come back. Maybe she should call in a few days when he had plenty of time to be sorry.

She wondered if Tommy missed her. Tears overflowed so suddenly, she sniffled. She wiped them away quickly, but Matt had seen.

"You cryin'?" He sounded mad.

She shook her head and dug in her pocket for a tissue.

"You lie to me, I'm gonna get mad, Katie. What the hell you cryin' for?" The van swerved onto the shoulder as he looked at her instead of the road.

Kathy wiped her nose. "I'm not really crying. I'm just sad about leaving Tommy." She looked out the window and sniffled again.

Matt was quiet a moment. Then, in a gentler tone, he said, "I'm sorry about Tommy, but your pa didn't leave me no choice. Nope, he was real sure about that. 'You go on and get out right now,' he said. 'She can't never come back, so go on, get outta here and don't let me ever see either one of you again.' "

He was watching her with quick, darting glances, but she didn't turn. She wasn't sorry about being with him, she just hadn't gotten used to the idea of never seeing her father and Tommy again.

"You hungry?" Matt asked.

That snapped her out of gloom. "I could eat a bear."

"We'll stop at a restaurant for breakfast. We should be comin' to a town soon."

Breakfast in a restaurant. And he'd promised to buy her clothes. Even if she only got a few things, it would cost plenty.

"Matt?"

"Yeah?"

"Do you have any money? I haven't got a dime."

"I got paid yesterday."

"What about your job?"

"I'm not going back."

"But this is Rasmun's truck—"

"He gave it to me."

"Gave it to you?"

Matt's brow furrowed. "Well, no. I'm buying it from him. He said it was okay to send the money when we got settled and I had a job and all."

Kathy shook her head in wonder. Matt had been so sure of himself and of her, he'd been able to convince Mr. Rasmun to trust him. It seemed incredible.

They came to a town an hour later. It was a single street, with a grocery, a feed store, a hardware, and a small cafe where they had the breakfast Matt promised. Afterward they bought bread, cold cuts, milk, and doughnuts in the grocery store before setting out again.

They drove all day. Matt turned onto a dozen different roads, so it was hard to keep track of directions. Once when she asked him where they were, he said it didn't matter. At times he hummed softly or broke into off-key singing that made Kathy laugh. She sang along, trying to keep him on pitch, but the more he tried the worse he was. They both laughed until their jaws ached. As the sun began to sink behind the western mountains, purple shadows crept across the road. It would be dark soon. They rode between a long stretch of towering pines that spilled right onto the edge of a town. Matt slowed.

It was big enough to have a mercantile store and a Rexall Drug. Matt turned onto a side street and parked. They shopped the Rexall first. Kathy worried about spending too much, but Matt insisted she pick out everything she needed. The bill came to twelve dollars and thirty-two cents. Matt paid with a twenty.

In the mercantile store, Kathy made her selections carefully, still hesitant about the cost. Two sets of underwear and socks, a sweat shirt, a T-shirt with a picture of the Grateful Dead, and a pair of jeans she hoped would fit because she didn't want to try them on with Matt pacing back and forth waiting for her. They were the last customers in the store. The skinny clerk with steel-rimmed glasses was already turning off lights up front.

"Hurry up, you two," he called. "Closing time."

"You got everything?" Matt asked.

Kathy nodded and laid the things on the counter. She'd added up the prices in her head and they came to more than thirty dollars. She wondered if Matt had that much.

The man rang up the sale. Matt pulled four crumpled tens from his pocket and dropped them on the counter. The clerk counted out the change and slammed the register shut. He flipped another switch that darkened the store except for a few night bulbs that left an eerie gloom. He opened the front door, waiting for them to go.

Kathy knew from Matt's expression he didn't like being put out like that. She slipped her arm through his and kissed his cheek.

"Thanks, Matt. I never had so many new things all at once. I feel like a princess."

He looked at her. "No kidding?" He grinned and began to whistle softly.

Kathy wondered how much money he had left. How long would it last them? *Them.* Matt was right, no matter what happened she'd never go back to Pa.

Still whistling, Matt ushered her into the van with a bow that made her giggle. When he went around to the driver's side, instead of climbing in, he reached behind the seat for the athletic bag.

"Back in a minute," he said. "I forgot something." He ran off in the darkness.

He was back in less than five minutes. He was still holding the athletic bag, but in his other hand he had a bright red tote. How in the world had he gotten the clerk to open the door for him again?

Matt gave her the tote bag. "To keep your stuff in, like I promised."

She felt the smooth vinyl. When Matt got behind the wheel, she leaned across the engine box and kissed him.

"It's super! Thanks!"

Grinning, he started the van. "You really like it?"

"I love it, Matt. I just love it!"

Still grinning, he put the van in gear and pulled away from the curb, tires squealing.

13

As soon as Elliot saw Harriet's somber expression, he knew the news wasn't good. She didn't mince words.

"A Conservation Department worker found a car up near Stampede Dam this morning. Someone crashed it into the gate, then walked away." She took a deep breath. "There was a body in the trunk. No wallet but they traced the registration. The man lived in Grass Valley. His wife says he went to pick up a pump in Yuba City yesterday and didn't come home last night."

The air-conditioned concourse stretched to eternity. Elliot felt like a condemned man walking the last mile. "Briggs?"

"A fingerprint man is on the way from Sacramento."

Elliot clenched his teeth so hard, pain shot from his jaw to temple. Stampede Dam was only a few miles from the cabin. "How was the guy killed?"

"Strangled." Harriet looked at him. "It doesn't necessarily mean Briggs is on another murder spree, Elliot. He has to keep moving, and stealing cars is the easiest way. The old guy probably put up a fight."

"Christ, do you really think Briggs got to the cabin?" Elliot's voice choked.

She pulled out of the parking space. "I wish I could say no, but it seems more likely all the time. His fingerprints were on both trucks, so we know he got as far as Yuba

71

City. An unrelated car theft and murder could be coincidence but it's a real long shot.''

Elliot pressed a hand over his eyes. If Briggs had gotten as far as Stampede Dam, he could walk to the cabin. And now Kay and Jeff were gone, so was the car. Elliot stared out the window without seeing the feeble burst of autumn on the dry mountainsides. Thinking about the possibility of Briggs being with Kay and Jeff made his gut ache.

The sheriff's car was parked in the clearing. Davies was a big man with a firm, hard build that didn't support an ounce of fat. He shook hands with Elliot.

''Mr. Pier, if we'd known your wife was Kathy Gerrett, we could have protected her before—''

Elliot cut him off. ''Kay's past is nobody's business but ours.''

''If Briggs came here, it's police business now,'' Davies said sharply. ''Do you have photos of your wife and the boy?''

Elliot took a studio portrait from his briefcase. It showed a smiling Kay with an arm around Jeff. It had been his Valentine gift from them.

''I'll have copies made. The boys at highway patrol will need them.'' Davies gave Elliot an appraising look. ''I'll level with you, Pier. We don't have the slightest idea which way Briggs is headed now. *If* he came here.''

Elliot glanced at the left-behind suitcases, Jeff's swim fins, and the Dodgers baseball cap on the doorknob. His chest burned. ''He was here.''

''How'd he know how to find your wife, Mr. Pier?''

Elliot jerked around. ''What the hell is that supposed to mean?''

Davies was unruffled. ''Was your wife in contact with Briggs while he was in prison?''

''No!''

''Could she have written him without you knowing it?''

''She wasn't writing to Briggs behind my back. She hated

his guts. Can you blame her?'' Davies's accusation was obscene.

"Briggs apparently knew she got married."

"A lot of people knew. We didn't go out of our way to publicize it, but we didn't hide it either."

"What about this place?"

"What about it? I had it long before I ever met Kay."

"Is the deed in your name?"

"Joint tenancy now." Elliot saw the direction of the questioning. If Briggs had located the cabin, he knew a lot about Kay's life since her release from prison. How?

"It would be recorded with the county," Harriet said.

Davies gave her a patient smile. "How do you figure Briggs got into the county records?"

Ed Viemont intervened. "You know how prisons are today, Chuck." His tone was the placating one of old friends who had argued the issue before. "They've got access to the library system and that lets them network right up to just about any level they want. Hell, half of them are studying law and writing their own appeals." He glanced at Elliot. "Didn't the *Times* do a series about a year ago on education in rehabilitation?"

Elliot was grateful to Viemont for sidetracking Davies. Briggs sure as hell had found out somehow where Kay was. It was frightening to think he'd kept close tabs on her life—their lives. Even scarier was the possibility that he planned his escape for the purpose of coming here. Sweat oozed between Elliot's shoulder blades and dampened his shirt.

Davies wasn't ready to give up. "Assume Briggs found out the way you say, Ed. How do you explain him knowing Mrs. Pier was here at the cabin and not home in L.A.?"

The question hung in the air like a poised hummingbird. Elliot swallowed hard. There it was, out in the open, like a flasher on Hollywood Boulevard: naked and obscene. Briggs had come directly here, with no detours to check the house in L.A. He'd *known* Kay was here. Davies's questioning glance slid around the group.

"I don't know," Elliot said helplessly. "He could have phoned the *Times* and found out I'm on vacation. I'll be damned if I know how he did it, but that's not important. Finding Kay and Jeff is. Briggs is a psycho, and he's kidnapped my wife and child—" His voice broke.

"Briggs is only dangerous to people who cross him," Davies said.

Elliot's head jerked up and his eyes were wild. "Damn it, Sheriff—"

Harriet put a restraining hand on Elliot's arm. Davies looked smug.

"It's my duty to notify the state authorities that Briggs probably came this way, and that he may not be traveling alone anymore. I'll let them draw their own conclusions about whether or not he's got hostages." Davies walked out, his footsteps heavy on the porch, then fading as he crossed the clearing. The police radio cackled as he put through his call. Elliot pounded his fist savagely.

"Take it easy, Elliot," Ed said. "Davies is an arrogant son of a bitch, but he's a good cop. No matter how much his questions bug you, you're going to have to face them eventually. He's not the only one who's going to ask them."

"It's stupid and impossible! Kay would no more go off with Briggs—" Elliot raked his fingers through his hair and paced to the window to look out at the police car. Ed was right. He was going to have to face a lot of things. He took a deep breath.

"Harriet's got coffee in the kitchen," Ed said. "We could all use a cup." He herded Elliot ahead of him. Seated at the table with steaming coffee in front of them, Ed put it succinctly. "If Briggs escaped and made his way here in less than forty-eight hours, we have to concede he knew what he was doing. For the moment, let's ignore how he managed it and try to figure out why. What's he after? Where's he headed now?''

Elliot rubbed his forehead, frowning. "There's no telling."

"There has to be," Ed insisted. "If he broke out on impulse, he'd run as fast as he could. He wouldn't hamper himself with a woman and child." Ed studied the dark liquid in the mug. Faint sounds of the deputies searching the hill behind the cabin filtered down intermittently. Davies had told them to look for anything significant, including bodies or fresh graves. That possibility hadn't occurred to Pier yet.

"You think he's headed someplace specific?" Elliot asked.

"Could he be retracing his path? Looking for his past?" Harriet was pensive as she leaned on her elbows.

Elliot scowled. "Blue Canyon? I don't think so. It represents everything Briggs ran away from. He'd think of it as another prison, not a refuge. He hated the place. Unless he's completely irrational, he has to know he'd be recognized there faster than anyplace else. Small towns don't change that much in eleven years."

"Someplace else then?" Ed persisted.

"They covered six states."

"Where'd they stop?"

"Along the road. Cheap motels—"

"Where?"

Elliot shrugged. "Missoula, Boise, Yellowstone, Barstow. I don't remember." He and Kay never talked about it anymore. In therapy, she'd faced enough of her fears so she could pick up the pieces and put together a new life, but there were dark corners too painful to probe. Her guilt about leaving home had never been exorcised. Together they had learned to avoid subjects that might push Kay back into the serious depression she'd suffered during the early part of her prison term.

Jeez, what kind of hell was she going through now?

Elliot closed his eyes. At the trial, a police psychiatrist testified that Briggs was a paranoiac. Elliot dredged his memory for the testimony.

"Briggs grew up in a hostile environment that left him without feelings of remorse or guilt about striking back at family, his peers, casual acquaintances, or even strangers he meets in the course of living. 'They' are out to get him. So he puts himself completely apart from rules or regulations that govern the rest of the world. He takes what he wants when he wants it. He punishes or destroys anyone or anything that threatens him, and he does it with the conviction that it's perfectly right for him to do so."

A crazy. A mad killer with no respect for human life. According to the psychiatrist, Briggs had not been looking for recognition from the world. His need was far more simple: love. He wanted to be loved. His casual friendship with Kay was distorted in his mind to undying passion. Briggs was convinced from the start, probably from the first time he talked to her, that she loved him as totally as he believed he loved her. He killed her father because the old man refused to let her go for a ride that night.

QUESTION: Why did you go to the Gerrett house that night?
ANSWER: To take Katie for a ride.
QUESTION: Did she ask you to come?
ANSWER: She promised to go for a ride with me.
QUESTION: When did she say that?
ANSWER: We talked about it a lot. I promised I'd come and get her.

Promised. Promises were important to Matt Briggs. He used to make Kay promise all sorts of things, and he'd hold her to them. *Promise.* He made her promise to wait for him the day he was captured. *Promise.* He made her promise to wait, and he promised to come back for her.

"Jesus!"

"What is it?" Harriet looked at him with concern.

Elliot's expression was agonized. "Briggs had a pathological need for reassurance that Kay wouldn't leave him. He'd say, 'Wait for me. Promise.' If she didn't, he slapped her around until she did. That's why she was too scared to try to escape until she heard he'd been captured."

Harriet picked up his train of thought. "And you think he's collecting that promise now?"

"It would account for why he kept track of her. It couldn't have been easy to find out all he knows. Like us being here, not in L.A. This is the first time I've ever taken my vacation in September. He had to be right on top of every move we made. It was a lousy break that Kay and Jeff were alone when he got here. My going to New York made it easier, but he'd have found a way no matter what."

"He probably would have killed you. You'd be like Kay's father: someone who didn't want Kay to go with him."

And maybe Jeff would be dead like Tommy, Elliot thought sickly. "The bastard! I'll kill him."

Harriet put a hand on his shoulder. "I'll get you some hot coffee." She went for the pot. As she came back, Sheriff Davies returned and stood in the doorway.

"We got a report on your car. It was parked at a red curb on a street in Twin Falls. The beat cop who ticketed it this morning walked in just as the APB came in."

"Twin Falls, Idaho?" Elliot demanded.

"That mean something to you?"

"God, I hope not. It could be on the way to Yellowstone."

Davies rubbed his square chin. "His prints are being wired. If they match, we can assume your wife is with him. They've crossed a couple of state lines now. That makes it a federal case.''

Elliot barely heard. All he could think about was Yellowstone Park and the horror Briggs had left behind there once before.

14

Shivering, Kay huddled in the corner as Matt turned on the heater, which whirred in fitful blasts. The car was a Toyota, far from new, the kind that would pass unnoticed anywhere. A clone of hundreds of others. Matt drove with nervous energy that did nothing to improve his skill, but on the desolate rural road there was little danger of a collision. They were alone in the night.

Exhaustion overcame her, and her eyes drooped. She dozed restlessly, haunted by menacing shadows that brushed her dreams. She woke with a start as the car bumped across gravel and slowed to a stop. Matt turned off the ignition. She looked around quickly, but the landscape merged into the darkness as the headlights went off, giving her only a faint impression of bleak, black hills and a night sky without moon or stars.

Matt got out. She listened to his steps on the gravel, then the sound of him urinating. Cautiously, she felt the ignition, but keys weren't there. A moment later Matt opened the door beside her.

"Get out if you want," he said. When she glanced nervously at Jeff, Matt grunted. "He's okay." He thumped his hand on the edge of the door.

The cold air made Kay realize how long she'd been cooped up. Alone, she could have made a dash for freedom, welcoming the darkness, but instead she took care of her needs and hurried back. Matt was in the back seat with Jeff.

"Get some sleep." His voice slurred with weariness.

"Matt—"

"Shut up. I'm tired."

She sat shivering. Could she make a run for it and find help before he woke? No, she couldn't leave Jeff. Sleep. She needed sleep. Her head lolled. Succumbing, she lay down, shifting so the seat buckles didn't stab. Sleep claimed her instantly.

When she woke, her back ached and her legs were stiff. She reached for Elliot, then sat up with a jolt as reality jarred her fully to consciousness. She scrambled up. The back seat was empty.

"Jeff—"

She yanked the door open, stumbling as she tried to stand on her numb legs. Clutching the door, she squinted in the predawn, searching. The bleakness she'd sensed last night surrounded her. Black, barren hills rolled to the distant magenta omen of sunrise. The road was empty.

"Jeff?" The sound was a terrified whimper. Where were they? Panicked, her gaze swept the undulating hills. *Jeff . . . Jeff . . .* Then she saw the two tiny figures out on the black terrain.

"Jeff!"

Weaving and stumbling, she tried to find a way down the embankment. Rocks slashed her hands like steel blades as she skidded on the seat of her jeans. When she reached a level spot, she pushed herself up, wiping her bloody palms. Pain shot through her ankle as she tried to find the spot where she'd seen Jeff and Matt. The sun broke over the horizon with a splash of gold. Then, suddenly, two figures came over a rise only a few yards away.

"Mommy, Mommy!" Jeff tried to run, but Matt jerked him back.

Kay fell to her knees and hugged her son. "Are you all right?"

"I had to go potty."

She sobbed against his sweater. They had been walking toward her all the time. She brushed away the tears, aware of Matt's angry stare.

"I was scared when I woke up and you were gone," she said finally. She still tasted the brassy terror as she got to her feet.

Matt ignored her and pulled Jeff toward the car. Modesty forgotten, Kay unfastened her jeans and squatted before she rushed after them. Matt had the trunk open and was reaching into a grocery sack. He took out a box of doughnuts and three small cartons of orange juice and set them on the bumper. He tore open a juice carton and pushed it toward Jeff. Jeff hesitated, then took it while Matt opened the doughnut box. Kay knelt beside Jeff as he stuffed a doughnut into his mouth with a grubby hand. His eyes were guarded and his body tense. She nuzzled his neck, then wiped powdered sugar from his face. His pants and shirt were wrinkled and his face streaked where tears had left muddy furrows. She gave him a quick squeeze.

"Leave him alone," Matt ordered. He motioned to the food. "Hurry up. We haven't got all day." He washed down his doughnut with juice.

Kay realized she was ravenous. She snapped open a juice carton and took a doughnut. Jeff reached for a second doughnut hesitantly, then, getting no reprimand, ate it quickly. Kay ate a second one and finished her orange juice. Matt held out the box to Jeff, who didn't look to his mother for approval this time as he took another doughnut. Matt shoved the last one toward Kay, then tossed the empty box in the trunk.

"This is a nice place," he said, glancing around. "It's lava. I read a book."

Lava. Kay dropped her empty carton into the trunk. There were lava beds near Blue Canyon. They couldn't have driven that far last night. Someplace else then. She tried to sound interested rather than desperate.

"Where are we?"

"It's a park. Do you know that flowers grow in lava?"

She shook her head. *Keep him talking.* "I don't know anything about volcanoes."

"My pa seen them a long time ago. He promised to take me." Anger honed his voice. He wiped the back of his hand across his mouth, then jerked his thumb at Jeff. "Finish that. We gotta go."

Jeff stiffened as though the spring controlling his fear had been rewound. He gulped the juice and put the carton in the trunk. He jumped back when Matt slammed the lid. When Matt ordered him into the car, Jeff moved toward the door obediently. Kay shuddered at the docile prisoner he was becoming.

When Matt held out the keys, she stalled. "Can I comb my hair first?"

He looked surprised, then smiled. "Your hair's like gold, Katie. I dream about it a lot." He put out his hand to touch it, and Kay cringed. His hand and the smile froze.

Oh, God, don't let him get mad—She forced an awkward laugh. "It's a mess. It's all tangled."

His expression softened. "Okay, but make it snappy." He walked around the car and stood by the open door.

Kay found her purse and perched on the driver's seat while she rummaged for her comb. Her fingers brushed the smooth leather of her credit card case. *Drop something. Let someone know we were here.* She glanced at Matt's reflection in the windshield. He was staring at her hair. She slipped one of the cards from the case and dropped it in her lap as she lifted the comb. The credit card burned against her jeans like a firebrand, but Matt's gaze didn't move. She began drawing the comb through her hair, tilting her head to work out the snarls as she kept Matt's reflection in view. He seemed hypnotized. Slowly, she relaxed her legs and let the card slide between her denimed thighs. It hit the ground with a plink. Jeff took a quick step and reached down to pick up the card. In panic, Kay dropped her purse over it and grabbed Jeff, pulling him onto her lap. She cupped his chin, holding his mouth firmly shut so he couldn't say anything as she began combing his unruly thatch.

"Here, let's see what we can do with you," she said with forced cheerfulness. She gave him a warning look as she patted his cowlick. His hazel eyes regarded her with a hurt expression. Matt's image shifted, and she turned quickly. "Can Jeff sit in back?"

"No. Right here." He touched the seat beside him.

She lifted Jeff across the wheel and Matt settled him on the seat. Kay closed her door and put the key in the ignition.

She hadn't realized they were only a dozen yards from the blacktop road. Matt said it was a park, but there was no sign of other cars or people. Her watch had stopped during the night, and there was no clock in the dashboard of the Toyota. It couldn't be much past six. Too early for tourists? Or some remote park that drew little traffic? She was sure she'd never been here before, but there were thousands of places she'd never been.

Was it possible that twenty-four hours ago she'd been helping Elliot get ready for his trip? *Oh, Elliot—*

They rode along the park for some miles. The black lava mounds stretched endlessly on one side of the road and a distant mountain range on the other. The only sign of life they encountered were occasional huge trucks thundering past in the opposite direction. The first highway sign she saw was a state marker. Idaho. The number meant nothing to her. Matt seemed to have memorized the route and didn't consult his map again. He was content to watch the scenery as though it were the only reason they were there. She felt like a circus performer on a tightrope without a safety net below. If she accepted Matt's silence, she and Jeff were helpless pawns. If she encouraged him to talk, she ran the risk of igniting his temper by some chance remark. Finally she summoned her courage.

"This is a pretty road." He didn't turn. She plunged ahead. "I've never seen lava beds before, not even the ones near Blue Canyon. Did you ever go there?"

He didn't answer except for a quick shake of his head.

"They're really something, aren't they? I mean these."

He looked at her then. "You like this place, huh?"

"Yes. It's so different. What book did you read?" *Keep him talking.*

"I forget. Just a book." Tightness edged back into his voice.

He doesn't want to be reminded of prison. She searched for neutral ground. "How did you know where I lived, Matt?" His gaze impaled her like a butterfly being added to a collection. Pride? Adoration? *Possession.*

"I know everything about you, Katie. I learned a lot of things in—" His fist clenched. "I had a lot of friends, guys who wanted to talk to me. Not like those stupid jerks in Blue Canyon. You know what they were like."

She nodded, encouraging him to go on.

"At first I didn't want to talk, but Juhnny wouldn't leave me alone."

"Johnny?"

"Juhnny, Juhnny. You know Juhnny. We used to talk about you all the time. He came to see me in the hospital."

She swallowed nervously, not taking her eyes from the road. "I didn't know you were sick."

"I'm okay now." Angrily.

A mental hospital? An aberration? Or had he really been ill? Was Juhnny a doctor or an inmate? Her mind whirled with the improbability of sorting Matt's ramblings.

"I'm glad you're better," she said.

He fell silent again. She tried to find another avenue into his thoughts. He was still mentally unbalanced, but what direction did his insanity lead? Where was he taking them? She flicked a glance at Jeff. He was subdued, hands folded in his lap as he stared at the air vent directly in front of him. He was already terrified of Matt, who had struck him, and now he didn't trust her anymore. He'd been trying to help by picking up the credit card. Instead of the smile his desire to help should have earned, she'd hurt his feelings. She was no longer the secure, comforting mother he'd always known. She wanted to reassure him, but maybe it was better this way. Silent, he wouldn't say the wrong thing and upset Matt. Her neck prickled as she thought of him walking placidly across the lava beds with Matt this morning.

Again, she tried to assess Matt's mood, then made another start. "What's the name of that park?"

His head jerked abruptly.

"The lava beds," she said quickly.

He shrugged. "I forget, but there's a big crater, and caves, and lots of wildflowers."

"I'll bet they're pretty."

"Yeah. Pretty." He was staring at her in a way that made her flesh crawl.

"Maybe we could stop and see them."

"We don't have time. We gotta get there."

There? A wave of dizziness made the road swim before her eyes. Her raw palms were fiery as she gripped the wheel. *There*—Her mind peeked through a dark doorway of the past momentarily before she was able to slam it shut.

15

They'd been sleeping in the back of the van for three nights. Kathy was stiff and sore. She felt miserable, and if that wasn't enough, Matt's moods zapped from cheerful to morose without warning. One minute he'd be laughing and singing, the next sullen and angry over something she said or did. Or didn't say or didn't do. It was getting so she was afraid to talk to him for fear of setting him off. Like today. They'd stopped in some tiny town on a back road in the middle of nowhere. Matt had said he was hungry, but when she started for the small cafe on Main Street, he flew into a rage, demanding to know if she thought he was made of money. He ordered her to stay in the van while he went and bought stuff for sandwiches, fruit juice, and potato chips. Kathy retreated into sullen silence.

What was wrong with wanting a decent meal and a comfortable bed? The excitement of being away from home was wearing off. Not that she still wasn't enjoying the freedom, but there was a limit. She stared at the deepening twilight and continued to punish Matt with silence.

"Hey!" he said suddenly. "Did you see that?" He pointed out at the bumpy blacktop. She shook her head without looking at him. "It was a coyote. Ran right across the road."

"It was probably a dog."

"It was a coyote."

She shrugged.

"You should be interested in things like coyotes. Bet you never saw one."

"I have, too. Plenty of them."

"Right on the road like that?"

"Sure. Besides, I didn't see this one. It *could* have been a dog." She didn't care if he liked it or not. But he didn't get mad. He changed the subject.

"You ever been in Idaho before?"

She shook her head. "I've never been more than forty miles from Blue Canyon until now."

"They got a lot of mountains and wild animals," he said. "Maybe we'll see a bear."

She shuddered and threw him a nasty look. He still didn't get mad. Maybe he was sorry he'd yelled about the cafe. Maybe she could talk him into staying someplace decent for a change.

"Let's stay in a motel tonight," she said daringly. She saw the little tic at the corner of his mouth, but she didn't care. "I can't sleep in the van another night! I get so cold my teeth chatter, and I'm sick of washing up in icy streams. I'll go without eating if I have to but I want to feel clean and rested."

"I ain't never let you go hungry, have I?" he demanded.

She shook her head and stared out the window again, pouting. What right did he have getting mad because she wanted to live like a civilized person? It was his fault, her being here and sleeping on a dirty piece of carpet with only a ratty blanket for cover. How could she be happy when she ached as if she'd spent the past few nights in a rock quarry?

The silence became ominous, but she wouldn't give in. She didn't care if he threw her out and just left her by the side of the road. She wished she were home. *Home . . . Pa . . .* She couldn't go home. If only she didn't feel so lousy. She closed her eyes and imagined the pleasure of a shower and shampoo. Her hair felt like greasy rope even though she brushed it hard every morning and night. How could Matt stand looking at her?

"Okay," he said suddenly. "We'll find a motel as soon as we get there."

She looked at him suspiciously. "You mean it?"

"Sure, why not? I'll look for one as soon as it gets dark." She wriggled close and kissed his cheek, feeling better instantly. A sign a while back said they were coming to Butte. There'd be plenty of motels there—and lights and stores and people! Maybe Matt would take her to a movie.

They stayed on the fringe roads around the city. Matt passed up three motels with bright neon signs that said they had vacancies. She was beginning to think he hadn't meant what he said at all when he turned into the Wee Rest. Kathy hid her disappointment when she saw the tiny office with a row of small cabins behind. She was hoping for a Holiday Inn or one of those big, bright places with its own restaurant. Well, she supposed as long as there was a bed and a shower it would be okay.

Matt went in to register and came back with a key. It was the last cabin in the row. He pulled the van around the side, then carried in their stuff. The room was barely big enough for the double bed, a dresser with a TV and lamp on top, and a wobbly armchair. Looking at the double bed, Kathy's cheeks flushed.

Matt opened the bathroom door and gave her a huge grin. "You said a shower, right?"

She nodded, then busied herself with the red tote bag, still wondering if he had any ideas about the bed. She heard him humming as he walked around examining the TV, the drapes, the pictures on the wall. When she carried her things to the bathroom, he watched from the doorway. She unwrapped two little bars of soap on the sink.

"Guess I'll go into town and look around. I'll pick out a nice place for us to eat, okay?"

Relieved, she said "Great."

"Wait for me, ya hear? I'll come back for you."

"Sure, Matt. I'm not going anywhere but into a nice hot shower."

He picked up his athletic bag. At the door, he looked back, and Kathy waved jauntily. A minute later she heard the van drive off.

Much later when she emerged from the steamy shower, she wrapped herself in a bath towel while she rinsed out her underwear and T-shirt. If they weren't dry by morning, she'd ask Matt to string up a line in the back of the van. Maybe they'd sleep late. She sure could use the extra rest. She turned on the TV and propped herself on the bed to watch *M.A.S.H.* The bed felt good. She didn't realize how tired she was. Blinking, she tried to keep her eyes open. She had to get dressed. Matt would be back soon. The soft pillows drew her down into a warm nest. She was aware of the news coming on, but her eyes were so heavy. She had to get up and put on some clothes . . . turn off the TV . . . From a great distance, she heard the newsman say something about a mercantile store in Cottonwood.

He stood in the dark doorway watching the lighted window. Most of the stores in town were already closed. He'd walked four blocks before he found what he wanted. A lighted moon-faced clock in the sporting goods store window showed it was two minutes past nine. The last customer was at the cash register where a clerk with a bulging stomach and sausagelike fingers was ringing up the sale. As the customer started out, Matt crossed the street and caught the door before it closed.

The fat man turned. "Sorry, mister, we're closed."

"I want a sleeping bag." Matt pointed to the camping gear at the back of the store.

The fat man hesitated, then shrugged. "Okay, but make it snappy." He began to tally the register.

Matt walked back and looked over the array of sleeping bags. Two were laid out beside a small tent as though waiting for people to slip into them. Two others were hung on the wall, their flaps pinned back so the quilted linings showed. Under the display, a bin was filled with rolled-up bags wrapped in plastic.

A section of overhead lights went off. The fat man called, "You'll have to hurry, mister. I want to get home."

"I can't make up my mind," Matt said without turning. He heard the clerk mumble irritably. Then his footsteps approached.

"What kind are you looking for? We've got some beauties in goose down." He leaned over to lift out one of the bags from the bin.

Matt's hand came out of the zippered bag and slashed. The fat man grunted as air whooshed out of him. His pig eyes bugged and his mouth opened. He looked down at the blood puddling on the shelf of fat before it streamed down his shirtfront. He clutched his belly as he saw the knife in Matt's hand. His face turned the color of suet. He tried to run, but Matt tripped him and sent him sprawling. The man landed like a small earthquake. When he tried to crawl away, Matt booted his rump and flattened him, then straddled him. The knife slashed again . . . and again . . . and again. . . .

Matt wiped the blade carefully on the fat man's shirt before putting it back in his bag. Then he zippered the windbreaker over his blood-spattered shirt. He selected one red and one green sleeping bag from the bin and jammed them under his arm. At the front of the store, he picked up the cash bag the clerk had readied and turned out the rest of the lights. He pulled the door shut behind him and tested the lock. Three blocks away, he went through the drive-through of a McDonald's for four Big Macs and two shakes before he drove back to the motel.

Standing behind the van in the dark, Matt stripped off the bloody shirt and jeans. The cool air made his skin crawl with goose bumps, and he felt a quick stirring under his Jockey shorts. Reaching into them, he turned toward the woods and began to pump. He had to breathe through his mouth so he wouldn't make any noise except to whisper, *"Katie . . ."* when he spurted with relief.

He put on clean jeans and a shirt, then rolled his bloody clothes and the empty cash bag in the old army blanket. Moving quietly, he walked a few yards into the dark woods and heaved the bundle as far as he could into the thick brush. Back at the van, he picked up the athletic bag and the McDonald's sack and let himself into the room.

The TV was on, but Katie was asleep. Her blond hair on the pillow was soft and shiny. He put the sack on the dresser, then turned off the TV and the light and undressed in the dark. Katie stirred but didn't wake when he crawled in beside her. Gently he curved his body to hers. Her skin was like silk. He fell asleep spooned against her.

16

The deputies found a place on the hillside where someone had stood a long time. The night dew hadn't penetrated the ground; the carpet of pine needles was scuffed. The spot afforded a good view of the back of the cabin and an angled glimpse of the front clearing. Backtracking through the woods, they found a faint trail for about three hundred yards, but it vanished where the rocky terrain met the timberline. Davies admitted that it showed someone had come or gone that way, no more. Still he stationed a man to make sure no one trampled the spot until the state authorities and the FBI had a chance to examine it more closely.

An all-points bulletin had gone out for Briggs: wanted and considered dangerous. Authorities in Twin Falls had compiled a list of stolen or missing vehicles, but so far there was no lead to the car Briggs had taken after abandoning the Oldsmobile. The man was a chameleon, changing coloration each time danger threatened. Despite his careless discard of cars when he finished with them, Briggs had a knack for picking replacements that weren't immediately missed. If it was luck, Elliot hoped it ran out soon.

The Twin Falls police had lifted prints from the Olds door handles, dash, and trunk lid that matched Briggs's. Having the last vestige of doubt erased didn't make Elliot feel better.

An unmarked car pulled into the clearing early in the

afternoon. A tall, rangy man with wire-rimmed glasses got out and came onto the porch. Elliot met him.

"Mr. Pier? I'm Herb Farmington, the resident agent with the FBI for this area. May I come in?"

Elliot pushed open the screen door. Farmington looked more like a benevolent minister making house calls than someone capable of tracking down an escaped killer.

"I'm sorry about your wife and son." Farmington extended his hand.

"Is there any word?"

Farmington shook his head. "Nothing but Briggs's prints on your car. Sheriff Davies says you think they might be headed for Yellowstone. Would you mind telling me why?"

Elliot sensed the same lack of confidence he'd gotten from Davies, and he had to hide his irritation. "I figure he's looking for something."

Farmington looked skeptical. "Something he hid?"

"Something he thinks he had or should have gotten. Something he was promised. He's paranoid about promises." Elliot explained his theory.

When he finished, Farmington asked, "Why Yellowstone?"

"Twin Falls is on a direct route from here." Elliot detected a glimmer of interest in the agent's expression. "Briggs wanted to go to Yellowstone that first time. It was something from when he was a kid."

Farmington was alert.

"He'd never been there before," Elliot went on, "but someone had promised to take him. His father, I think, but he never got around to it." Bits of the trial and hundreds of conversations with Kay eddied in a whirlpool of certainty.

"That was then. Why now?" Farmington persisted.

"I'm not sure, but there was something. I know it. I feel it."

"The Bureau can't deploy men on hunches."

"It's more than a hunch." Elliot's anger was oozing back. What the hell did Farmington and Davies want?

Farmington took a pack of cigarettes from his pocket and tapped one out. He put it between his lips and flipped a lighter. Blowing smoke, he said, "Suppose I buy the idea he's headed for Yellowstone. You think he's after something your wife promised that long ago?" There was a faint hesitation before "your wife," and Elliot's jaw tensed as he nodded. Farmington's expression didn't change. "Briggs isn't the brightest fugitive we've ever had to run down, but now he's got the crafty smarts of a con who's been inside for ten years. You agree?" Elliot nodded with the feeling of taking one step closer to a hidden trapdoor. Farmington puffed on the cigarette, then studied the growing ash like a crystal ball. "Assuming Briggs has a reason for wanting your wife with him, why would he take your son along?"

Stunned, Elliot said, "I don't think he planned it that way. Jeff was here and—"

"Why not leave him?"

An image of the man from Grass Valley stuffed in a car trunk flashed through Elliot's mind. In sudden panic, he envisioned a small, towheaded body lying in the woods. He glanced toward the window. "Have they—"

Farmington shook his head in what was supposed to be a reassuring gesture but came off almost as disappointment. Elliot's anger flooded back, and it was oddly comforting.

"I said it before, Farmington. I don't know what's going on inside the head of that looney. All I know is the bastard was here and now he's got my wife and son!"

"This particular 'looney' escaped from prison, stole at least three vehicles, and is on the run. Whatever he came here for has to be pretty important, wouldn't you say?" Farmington was so damned cool, Elliot wanted to throttle him. He swallowed his rage and nodded silently. Farmington went on. "I'm inclined to agree there's a connection with your wife. Briggs knew where to find her. That indicates a plan. But the child? The son of the man his old girl friend married? I don't think so, unless—''

Elliot was rigid. ''Unless what?''

''Someone important enough to Briggs might convince him to take the boy along.''

For a moment, Elliot missed the implication. He frowned, his mind racing. ''You mean Kay talked him out of hurting Jeff?''

''It's possible.''

More than possible. Kay would do anything to protect Jeff. Even go with a madman? If he threatened Jeff, yes.

''You see why it's important for us to know what Briggs is after. Personally I like your theory that he's headed for something, not just running. It explains a couple of things that don't make sense otherwise. But—'' He leveled a glance at Elliot. ''We've got to have more to go on than what you've given me. Can you think what this promise might be? The one you think is taking him to Yellowstone?''

Elliot paced, aware that Harriet and Ed were watching from the kitchen. They'd gone over the same ground all morning trying to find an answer, but he hadn't been able to dig it out of his subconscious. Harriet assured him it would come, like the name of a bit player you could visualize in a role but couldn't identify. *Don't try. It'll pop into your head when you least expect it. Talk about something else.*

''The Yellowstone killings were hard for Kay to come to terms with,'' he said. ''It was the first time she really knew Briggs was a killer.'' He looked squarely at Farmington, daring him to challenge. When the agent remained impassive, he was encouraged. ''Up until then she was too full of her own guilt about leaving home to wonder about his. When she found out he'd murdered those people, she went to pieces. They fought—physically. Briggs beat the hell out of her, all the while telling her she belonged to him and no one else was going to have her. He began listening to the radio then. That's how she found out about the other murders. First the store owner in that little town, then the guy in Butte—'' He snapped his fingers, glancing at Harriet, who gave him a quick smile. Butte, not Boise. ''And not least of all, her father and brother. It was in all the broadcasts by then. Kay's guilt was unbearable. She'd spent a week with Briggs and not known he'd killed the only two people she had in the world. Sure, she hated her father. She'd wished him dead so many times, it had come true. Or so she thought. That's why she laid the heavy guilt trip on herself, not because she'd been Briggs's partner the way he testified.'' He stopped pacing and looked at Farmington. ''Would you believe it if I told you Briggs was impotent when it came to physical contact with a woman? He couldn't get it up with her.''

Farmington pursed his lips. ''That's a direct contradiction to his trial testimony.''

''He's psychotic, damn it! The D.A.'s office didn't want to risk an insanity plea so Briggs could walk after a few years!'' Reporters had picked up the rumor but no official statement had ever been made.

After a few moments Farmington said, ''What if I accept Briggs's impotency? Then what?''

Elliot went on. ''Kay never slept with him. They shared the same bed or sleeping bag or whatever the hell, but there was never any physical penetration. Briggs lived in a makebelieve world where they were lovers of undying passion. Maybe he got his kicks from the act of murder, I don't know. Kay never saw him masturbate but it's highly likely.''

''It's often the pattern with this type. If we accept your wife's version of the story, where does it take us? What does it have to do with Yellowstone?''

Elliot tried to organize his hopscotching thoughts. ''I'm not sure, but a buzzer goes off inside my head every time Yellowstone comes up. Something happened there, I'm sure of it. It was the start of their hard running and Kay's real terror. Up until then she was a kid on a lark. She believed her father wouldn't let her come home and she had no place else to go. After Yellowstone, she didn't want to stay with Briggs but she was trapped. He knocked her around on the slightest provocation from then on. And he made her promise all sorts of things. Those promises were damned important to him.''

"What kind of promises?''

Elliot made an impatient gesture, still groping for the elusive. "To walk with him. To eat eggs for breakfast. Anything. Always to wait for him when he went out. It was an obsession. If she didn't say yes, he hit her until she did. I'm sure there was some promise in Yellowstone that he's never let go of all these years.''

"So he came back for her?'' It was only half questioning.

"It has to be. Damn it, Briggs came straight here when he escaped. Somehow he kept track of her and knew where to find her. He wanted *her,* no one else, so it's got to be some promise he's never forgotten.''

Farmington was quiet a moment, then said, "Your theory doesn't do much for the idea of his taking your son along. A child couldn't have been involved in that old promise.''

Elliot's concentration broke as if Farmington had chopped it with an ax.

"Your wife must be a convincing talker.''

Elliot realized what Farmington was saying: if Kay had convinced Briggs to take Jeff along, was she an innocent hostage or a willing accomplice?

God, it was starting all over again.

17

Matt took over the driving about midday when Kay complained of exhaustion. He'd fallen silent after the brief flurry of talk about the lava park, and she hadn't been able to think of another safe topic to risk bringing up. Jeff had been quiet, too, confused and pouting over the credit card incident. But now, as the day wore on, he was growing restless. She slipped her arm around him reassuringly. Matt shot her a quick, angry look, but she turned her face to the window and pretended not to notice.

Shortly after noon they passed through a hot, dusty little town, where Kay glanced hopefully at the few people on the street and open shop doors, but the car drew no attention. Near the edge of town they passed a parked police car. Kay's heart leaped, but the uniformed officer didn't glance up as they went by.

They were invisible. Tourists . . . a family out with a purpose . . . just another car moving along the highway. . . . To where?

Past and present mingled torturously. Kay felt herself slip to the edge of the black abyss she'd tried so hard to blot from her life. She was being punished. There was no escape. Glancing at Jeff, she saw golden-haired Tommy, who had depended on her and trusted her . . . and whom she had betrayed. She closed her eyes and leaned against the window, letting the sun flush her face. *It can't happen again . . . it mustn't . . . oh, God, help me . . . Elliot—*

"What'd you say?"

She jerked up, alarmed because she didn't realize she'd spoken aloud. She shook her head as she tried to clear the cobwebs from her brain. Matt was glancing nervously from the road to her. The car swerved, rocking momentarily as the wheels dug into the soft shoulder. The tires whined as Matt brought the Toyota back onto the blacktop.

"I didn't say anything," Kay said quickly.

"You did!" His foot hit the brake. The car squealed and Jeff flew forward. Kay grabbed him. Trembling, she pulled him onto her lap.

"I—I mean—I didn't mean to say anything. I was wondering aloud." She swallowed nervously. "I was still thinking about those lava beds. How they were formed and all. Sometimes I wish I had studied more, like you." She was babbling. "I read in the paper about that volcano in Hawaii, the one that keeps erupting. I just can't imagine volcanoes here, right in the middle of the United States. Are there more?"

Matt leaned back, letting up on the brake and touching the accelerator. The car began to move again.

"Sure. I read a lot. You'd be surprised what I know."

"Where—where are the other volcanoes?"

He gave her a superior grin. "Lots of places. Oregon, Washington, California. Near the mountains. Earthquakes come from volcanoes."

She fixed a smile as he talked about the underground movement of the earth and pressure from gases that finally broke through the surface. It was obvious he'd read without really understanding, but she didn't interrupt. As long as he was calm, she and Jeff were in no immediate danger. When Matt fell silent, she sensed he'd exhausted his knowledge, but his anger had evaporated. He was back on an even keel.

Why was he so interested in volcanoes? she wondered. They hadn't stopped at that park last night by chance. He knew exactly where it was and had planned to stop there.

Now he was talking about mountains. She couldn't look in any direction without seeing a range. They'd left the Sierra, she was sure of that. The Rockies then. Idaho and the Rockies. She tried to visualize a map. The Rocky Mountains began far north of the United States in Canada or Alaska and ran all the way down to Mexico. Through Idaho. Through—She jerked up as though Matt had struck her. Sweat beaded on her temples and she pressed her fingertips to the pounding pulse there.

Frightened, she searched for a highway sign. She was wrong. They'd gone east from Blue Canyon. Not north. She was safe as long as they kept heading north. Oh, God, they'd been on so many roads she couldn't remember. She didn't want to remember!

18

When she woke, she snuggled into the warm, comfortable bed. Smiling, she started to stretch but drew back when she touched naked flesh close to hers. The towel she'd wrapped around herself last night was a tangled lump under her hip. She realized she was naked as a newborn chick—and the warm flesh was Matt's.

Moving cautiously, she turned to look at his sleeping form. His arm thrown over the covers was bare, his shoulder and smooth chest naked. She could feel the heat of his entire body beside her.

Carefully she slid out of bed and tiptoed to the bathroom, closing the door quietly. She hadn't heard him come back last night, hadn't heard him get into bed. Had he wanted to make love? She saw her flushed reflection in the mirror and realized *she* wanted to. After all, she was his girl, wasn't she? It wasn't so wrong doing it with someone who wanted to marry you, was it? Of course it was wrong. Not until you got married, her mother had told her before Tommy was born. Not that Kathy didn't know how babies were made. Living on a ranch, you knew that before you went to school. But even if babies were made the same way as calves and colts and puppies and kittens, there was a big difference, Ma said. You had to be married so there was a home and a mother and a father for a baby. Like her and Pa and Kathy and the new baby that would be there soon. A happy home . . .

Happy. Kathy grimaced at the face in the mirror. She wanted a lot better than her mother ever had. Working from sunup until after dark. Jumping whenever Pa said something, afraid of her own shadow, doing what she was told even when she was so tired she was ready to drop. Tired enough to die.

The image in the glass blurred, and Kathy rubbed her eyes furiously. She ran water in the sink and held a cold washrag to her face. She'd have a lot more than Ma ever did. Just you see, Pa. Matt loved her and wanted to take care of her. Didn't he get this motel last night just because she asked for it? Someday she'd have a nice house with a yard. Not too big so she had to plant and weed all the time. Not a ranch. That was definite. Not a ranch. She'd live in a city, with neighbors and maybe a park to walk in or stroll with the baby carriage.

Blushing again, she turned away from the glass. Matt had gotten right into bed beside her. If she'd been awake, would he . . . ? She felt the underwear and shirt she'd hung over the towel rack and was relieved to find them dry. She put them on. She'd find a place to get coffee and surprise Matt when he woke up. Smiling, she tiptoed back to the bedroom and put on her jeans. Then she slid her hand into the pocket of Matt's jeans, which were in a crumpled heap on the floor. She was astonished at the wad of bills. After all his yelling about money! There was more than two hundred dollars in tens and twenties and fives. She took two singles and pushed the rest back, then let herself out quietly.

There was a cafe in the next block. She ordered coffee and doughnuts to go. Back at the motel, she discovered the door was locked. She hadn't thought to take the key, so she had to knock.

The bed creaked. She heard soft, quick footsteps. Matt's voice was close. "Yeah?"

"It's me, Matt. Let me in."

The door opened a crack as he peered out. Then it jerked back abruptly. He grabbed her and pulled her inside.

"Where the hell were you?" He slammed the door and shoved her against it.

"I went out for coffee. Matt, you're hurting me!" His fingers were a tight band on her arm and the doorknob was digging into her back. Matt's hand came out of nowhere and struck her so hard, her head bounced against the door. Her cheek stung and her head was ringing. Angry tears spilled as she tried to pull away, but his hand was too quick. He hit her again.

"Matt—please—" she sobbed. She tried to raise her arm to ward him off and was surprised to find she was still clutching the sack. "Coffee," she said helplessly. "It's hot—"

His face froze in the twisted expression as if they were playing statues. Slowly, his hold relaxed. When he stepped back and sat on the edge of the bed, she realized he was naked.

"You promised to wait," he said petulantly.

Of all the dumb—She swallowed her anger rather than face his again. "I only went for coffee." She moved cautiously, averting her eyes as he pulled on his shorts. She busied herself prying the plastic lids off the cups. She saw the grease-stained McDonald's bag on the dresser. He never planned to take her out to dinner. He had some nerve getting mad.

"I brought burgers last night. You were asleep." The anger was easing from his voice.

Without turning, she said, "I was beat. I slept like a log." She guessed it really didn't matter about dinner. She was glad he hadn't woken her. As she unwrapped the doughnuts, he came up beside her. She saw in the mirror he was wearing only his shorts. She kept her gaze fixed on the coffee cups.

"I slept good too." His anger was gone. Kathy raised

her eyes and saw he was watching her. He smiled. "You washed your hair." He put his hand up and stroked it very gently. "I like your hair this way, Katie. It's like a gold waterfall in the sunlight."

Embarrassed by the unexpected compliment, she sipped her coffee. "I got doughnuts, too. They're still warm." When he reached for one, his arm touched her breast. A tingle jolted through her. Matt took a bite of doughnut.

"Good," he said with his mouth full. He picked up the other cup of coffee, blowing on it before he sipped. "You get the stuff together while I take a shower. We gotta get going."

"It's early."

"We gotta go," he said emphatically. The bathroom door closed. A moment later the shower thrummed.

She finished her coffee and doughnut while she gathered up their things. Matt's shirt was over the chair. Funny, she was sure he'd been wearing a blue one last night, not a white one. She shrugged and left it where it was. When she had everything in a neat pile, she made the bed. She was straightening the spread when he came out of the bathroom, his damp hair clinging to his forehead. He rubbed the faint haze on his chin.

"I don't have time to shave. I'll do it tomorrow." Glancing at the bed, he shook his head. "You're not supposed to do that. They got maids."

She'd done it out of habit. "I forgot." She hadn't known. She'd never been in a motel before.

"Got everything?" He pulled on the white shirt and his jeans. When she nodded, he gulped the last of his coffee and tossed the cup into the wastebasket. "Let's go."

In the van, Kathy noticed the sleeping bags immediately. "They're fantastic! Where'd you get them?"

"You like them? They're goose down."

She ran her hand over the silky, smooth shells. She'd never felt anything so soft. Goose down. Expensive. She gave him a big grin.

"I picked the red one for you," he said.

"It's pretty. Thanks, Matt." No more lumpy sofa pillow and dirty blanket. She settled in the seat as Matt started the engine. "It'll be like a real camping trip now," she said. "Where are we going? Where are we going camping, Matt?"

"How about Yellowstone Park? My pa promised to take me there someday. Yeah, let's go to Yellowstone." He backed the van out, narrowly missing a small pine at the edge of the drive. Kathy didn't even notice.

19

Farmington left without promising anything more than to keep in touch.

"He doesn't believe me," Elliot said. He sank onto the couch wearily.

"He listened," Ed Viemont said. "He wasn't overly enthusiastic, but you made him stop and think. Don't write him off completely."

Elliot gave a wry smile. "First I have to get his attention, huh? He's got red tape instead of arteries. Well, I'm not going to sit around waiting for Mr. Federal Bureau of Investigation to make up his goddam mind about whether he should follow up the only lead we've got."

Harriet gave him a worried look. "We know how you feel, Elliot, but we are speculating."

"I know I'm right. Briggs is headed someplace. It's got to be Yellowstone. If I could only remember—" He pounded his brow, then got to his feet. "I'm going to Yellowstone."

Harriet put her hand on his arm. "Give Farmington a little time."

"Time is the one thing I can't give anyone! Every minute Kay and Jeff are with Briggs, the more danger they're in, the closer he may be to doing something violent."

Harriet stood her ground. "Assume you're right, suppose you find them? What if Jeff spots you and does the absolutely normal thing for a kid that age? Suppose he yells, 'Daddy!' and tries to run to you?''

Elliot paled and chewed his lip. Weakly he said, "I'll have to be sure I see them first." He looked from Harriet to Ed. "I don't know how, but I'll figure it out as I go along."

Ed pushed himself up from the cushioned armchair. "I don't have a vote in this discussion, but I'll stick in my oar anyhow. Harriet's right, Elliot. It could be a mistake not leaving it to the experts." He put up a hand quickly as Elliot opened his mouth. "She's trying to keep you from running off half cocked. Neither of us is going to stop you. In your place, I'd do the same, but I have a suggestion. Tell Farmington. He may be able to put you in touch with someone up there to call if you need help."

Elliot considered the idea, then said, "Okay."

"You can call from my place," Harriet said. "Get some things together. You'll need warm clothes."

In the jeep, Harriet informed Elliot she was going with him. He shook his head. "Thanks, Harriet, but this is something I have to do alone."

"You can't," she said emphatically. "Ed and I talked it over while you were packing. Looking for them on your own is impossible. What happens if you find them? How can you be sure they'll stay put while you get help? Having me along will double the number of miles you can cover. The park is huge. They could be anywhere."

He couldn't let her get involved more deeply, but neither could he argue with her logic. Seeing his hesitation, she went on.

"I know Yellowstone. Wayne and I spent a lot of time up there. I can set us up with a camping rig so we'll look like tourists. It'll make it easier to move around. If Briggs went through Twin Falls, he's probably headed for the Teton or West Yellowstone entrance. I suggest we fly to Bozeman and go straight to park headquarters at Mammoth. We're going to need the rangers in this."

Elliot realized how practical Harriet's idea was. "Okay. Thanks, Harriet. But one thing—you don't go anywhere near Briggs when I find him."

She gave him a rueful smile. "I wasn't planning to."

At the house, Harriet packed while Elliot called Farmington. The FBI man warned him not to interfere and ordered him to stay at the cabin. Elliot hung up angrily, then immediately called a charter service to arrange a flight to Bozeman. Armed with her husband's old address book, Harriet made three calls before she found someone to put together the camping gear they needed.

Three hours later, when they touched down in Bozeman, they were met by a ruddy-complected teenager wearing a windbreaker emblazoned with the name of a local outfitter. He led them to a small motor home.

"There's food and fresh water. If you run out, the stores in the park are open," he told them. "Mr. Howell says just let him know where you want us to pick it up when you're done." The youth handed over the keys. A minute later he roared off toward town on a motorbike.

"Let's roll," Harriet said. "We've got some miles to cover before dark."

Elliot gave the interior of the motor home only a passing glance as he settled behind the wheel. He familiarized himself with the dashboard while Harriet fastened the door and settled in the copilot seat. Opening the glove box, she pulled out a handful of maps and brochures. She spread one open on her knees.

"Go east on 90 to Livingston, then south on 89 to the park."

The engine hummed smoothly. Elliot gave her a grateful smile. "Thanks, Harriet. I guess I was running off half cocked. I never would have thought of this."

She smiled. "Leave the mundane stuff to me and just get going."

He pulled out slowly, testing the vehicle's handling.

Harriet was quiet until they were on the interstate. Then she began to brief him on how the park system operated.

"There are five entrances. Mammoth is the north one, but once you're in the park, it's only an hour or two to the others. All rangers are coordinated out of the headquarters in Mammoth, but there are stations in several other places. There's a gate at each entrance. Anyone driving in has to buy a permit."

"Then Briggs will have to stop."

"Right, but it's pretty routine. You hand over your money and get a receipt. It's good for two weeks. You can go in and out through any gate as long as you show the ticket. If you want to use any of the campgrounds, that takes another permit. You buy it on site."

Elliot glanced at the alien landscape. A different world. A city boy all his life, he knew little about the outdoors except for the private oasis of the Sierra cabin. And that had always been a peaceful retreat from city woes rather than an escape to the woods. It had been change enough for him. And for Kay. They'd never considered camping trips. Ever since her journey through hell with Briggs eleven years ago, Kay was nervous about any kind of isolation. She shuddered at the thought of sleeping out or roaming the woods. He wondered if Briggs had a camper or van. He blocked out the thought. He'd go crazy imagining . . .

"There'll be a lot of activity in the park," Harriet said, glancing at him. "If they're already inside, it'll be like looking for a needle in a haystack."

"Except we have an idea of what he did before."

"You think he'll follow a pattern?"

"He's living the past, I'm sure of it."

She was silent a moment, then said, "It could be dangerous to anticipate him."

Elliot's face contorted with a spasm of pain. "It will be a lot more dangerous for Kay and Jeff if we don't."

* * *

They reached the north entrance as the sun fell behind the Gallatin Range and threw mauve shadows across the valley. Harriet directed him to the park headquarters building where they found the superintendent of park rangers expecting them.

"Freemont Bass," he said as he shook hands. "An FBI man called and warned us to be on the lookout for you. Frankly, Mr. Pier, the chances of spotting your wife and child are slim. Do you have any idea how many couples with a child come through here every day?"

Elliot wondered if Farmington had asked the ranger to try to stop him. "Are you married, Mr. Bass?"

The stocky, balding man nodded. "Believe me, we're doing everything we can. I've already alerted the gates. My people are writing down license numbers and descriptions of every vehicle that comes through with two adults and a child."

Harriet opened her bag and took out copies of the photographs Ed had wheedled from Davies and had waiting at the airport: Kay and Jeff in the smiling studio portrait, and Briggs's sullen prison ID shots. She handed them to Bass.

"I'll get these to the gates right away."

"It's possible they're already in the park," Harriet said. "We know they were in Twin Falls last night."

"I'll have today's duty roster take a look at these. Someone may recognize them."

"Briggs may be headed for a campground," Elliot said.

"We're full up," Bass said.

"I understand he has to sign in."

Bass nodded. "If he got in before the office closed, we'll have the registration on file. After hours he can drop the registration card in a box. They aren't picked up until morning. But we were filled by noon today, so there's not much chance of that."

Something nagged at a corner of Elliot's memory, but he couldn't pull it into focus.

"He's not likely to follow rules," Harriet observed.

Frowning, Elliot let the fragment fall into a slot. "When he was here before, he parked off the beaten track."

"It's against regulations, but we can't police every road," Bass said. "Once in a while we spot violators on early morning rounds, but there are probably ten who get away with it for every one we catch. Some of our roads are pretty isolated."

"My wife and kid's lives are at stake. Briggs is a murderer. The park must keep records. Which campground were those people killed at eleven years ago?"

Bass sat up, alert. "Are you talking about those crazy kids who . . . ?"

"Mad Dog Matt Briggs," Elliot barked. "Who did you think? What did Farmington tell you?"

"That a woman and child might be traveling with a man they were looking for—"

"Damn!" Not even kidnapped. *Traveling!*

Bass's face tightened. "You're saying Matt Briggs is the man . . . ?" He didn't need an answer. Elliot's face said it all. Bass reached for the phone. "Those people were killed at Bridge Bay. I'll have it checked immediately. Check back with me in an hour." He was already dialing.

20

The car began to sputter. Kay glanced at the gas gauge. The needle lay on E. They hadn't passed a station for miles. She looked at the rolling hills where sheep grazed. The hazy mountains to the west had stretched unbroken for miles, obliterated at times by dense stands of pine. Occasionally a fence attested to habitation, but she hadn't seen a house since they passed through a tiny town a half hour ago.

Jeff dozed fitfully, his head bowed so she couldn't see his face. For all Matt's demand for haste, he drove slowly. Still he picked the route with certainty. He turned from one county road to another as if the countryside were completely familiar. If they kept going north, they'd be out of Idaho soon. Beyond lay Montana, where she and Matt had been once before. She fought the specter of terror each fragment of memory roused.

The engine missed and the car slowed. Matt stomped on the gas pedal as a wheel bumped on loose gravel and the car rolled to a stop. Matt ground the ignition.

Jeff woke and whined. "Mommy?"

"Shh—it's okay, honey." Kay smoothed his warm, damp hair.

"Shut up, you stupid kid!" Matt shouted.

"I'm thirsty, and I gotta go potty." Jeff whimpered and rubbed his eyes.

"I said, shut up!"

Jeff cowered against his mother. Kay tightened her arm around him and pursed her lips in warning. Jeff's hazel eyes were frightened as he lowered his head again in mute silence.

"Stupid fuckin' car." Matt ground the starter again, then beat the steering wheel in rage. He jerked open the door and got out. Walking around the car, he kicked a wheel savagely, then stood in the road looking in both directions.

Kay bent to Jeff, whispering. "Be very quiet, darling. Don't say anything." He didn't look up. "But if I tell you to do something, do it fast, please?" She wasn't sure he heard. Matt was back at the door. All she could see was his middle and the crook of an elbow as he leaned on the top of the car. She snaked a hand into her purse and felt blindly for the credit card case as she watched the span of blue jeans. She slid a card out and quickly pushed it down by the door as Matt bent to reach under the seat. His hand came up with the butcher knife.

Jeff cringed. Kay pulled him close.

Matt looked at her. "Get out."

She fumbled for the door handle, not taking her eyes from him.

"Move!" He grabbed Jeff and jerked him across the seat.

Jeff screamed in terror. "Mommy!" Matt slapped him. Tears and an anguished wail exploded from Jeff. He struggled frantically but couldn't squirm from Matt's grasp. Matt hit him again. Kay scrambled out of the car quickly.

"I'm out, Matt, I'm out. Don't hit him—"

"Don't give me no fuckin' orders! Get over here!"

Weak-kneed, she hurried around the car. For a moment she thought she would vomit. She swallowed convulsively, blinded by tears. Matt shoved her onto the road.

"You stop the first car that comes along, you hear?"

She nodded. She could hear Jeff's soft snuffling. *Oh, God, let him be quiet.* She stumbled to the middle of the road and stared at the asphalt that shimmered under heat

waves. She prayed for a miracle. Glancing back, she saw
Matt perched on the edge of the seat. The knife gleamed
in the sun. She breathed deeply through her mouth. *Let a
car come . . . don't let him hurt Jeff . . .*

The sun beat like a relentless lava flow, yet she was
cold. Inside. Numb. She scanned the dipping road where
radiating heat cast ghost images. A raven flapped into sudden motion beside the road, startling her. The gentle sway
of the grass was the only other motion. She turned to Matt.

"There aren't any cars."

"We'll wait." He shifted the knife to the other hand,
watching it hypnotically as it glittered in the sunlight. Kay
bit her lip. *Get it away from him. Hit him over the head
and grab it.* She looked for a weapon, but there was nothing in the road. Would he let her walk? She took a tentative
step. His head jerked up. She pretended to search the distance as she took another step, holding her breath. Another
step . . . another. Her gaze raked the shoulders in search
of a rock or stick. There was only hard-packed dirt with a
scattering of tiny pebbles.

"Hey!"

She wheeled guiltily. Matt motioned her back. Could
she get the knife before he could turn on Jeff? Her mind
whirled. A sound penetrated her fear. She looked around
as a car materialized in the shimmering distance.

Matt ducked the knife and moved back so his face was
shadowed.

Kay raised her arms. Waving, she prayed the driver
would see her in time. The car was coming at a sedate
speed. Not a car. A pickup. It slowed, then pulled to a
stop behind the Toyota. A grizzled old man wearing a rail-
road cap leaned out the window.

"What's the trouble, young lady?"

"We—we ran out of gas." She glanced nervously at
Matt. He was out of the car, leaning on the open door.
There was no sign of the knife.

The old man pushed back his cap and scratched his bald

head. "Not many stations in these parts. You should have filled up back at Kilgore."

"You got a spare can?" Matt had come up behind her so quietly, Kay jumped.

The old man watched them curiously. "Nope."

"Where's the nearest station?" Matt demanded.

The old man cocked his head and squinted. "Fifteen miles back to Kilgore, twenty-three up t' Mack's Inn."

"You goin' that far?"

"Nope."

"How far you goin'?"

Kay heard anxiety building in Matt's voice. She looked at the old man and tried to telegraph the danger, but he was watching Matt warily.

"Seven miles."

"You live there?"

"Yup."

"You got gas there?"

"Nope."

Matt tensed. "You got a phone there?"

The man hesitated, then nodded. "I reckon I can give the little lady a ride so's she can call Ed at the Kilgore station. Mebbe he'll come out with some. Course, if he's alone, you may have to wait awhile."

Matt advanced a step so he was beside her. "She stays here. I'll go."

"I can't drive you back. I got hay to stack." He was watching Matt.

"I'll walk." Matt jerked his head toward the Toyota and said to Kay, "Wait in the car. I'll be back, you hear?" She started for the car quickly as Matt walked around the pickup. The old man grunted as the door opened.

Kay forced herself not to run. Behind her, she heard the door of the pickup slam. She slid behind the wheel of the Toyota and pulled the door shut. Jeff was hunched in a tight ball, his face hidden. She riveted her gaze on the rearview mirror. As soon as the old man and Matt drove off, she and Jeff would run. Not on the road. Across the fields. Hide. Fifteen miles back to the town. Her heart hammered like a faulty pump. Why didn't they go? She stared at the mirror, willing the old man to get the truck moving. She couldn't see him. Only Matt. Hunched sideways, his arm raised—

"Oh, God!" The knife slashed. Kay buried her face in her hands. "Oh, God, no, no, no!"

"Mommy, Mommy!" Jeff wailed.

She pressed her hands over her eyes. "Don't, Matt—for Godsake, don't—"

"Mommy!" Jeff's howl snapped her from her hysteria. They had to get away. She turned the key in the ignition frantically, pumping the gas pedal. Without warning, the door opened and Matt struck her arms a chopping blow, his face twisted with rage. There were red splatters across his shirt. Kay closed her eyes as nausea gagged her. Matt yanked out the key. The door slammed. Jeff's hysterical sobs forced her to open her eyes. Numbly, she took him in her arms and rocked him with quick, jerky motions. "Shh, shh, please be quiet. Shh, shh . . ."

The pickup door opened. Closed. Something clattered. Metal clinked. A shadow fell across the window as Matt moved behind the car. A soft gurgling sound. Gas pouring into the tank. Her mind numbed. The old man had lied. Lied. *Goddam it, don't lie to me. You lie, I'm gonna get mad!*

21

Matt's mood was cheerful again. Kathy wondered what triggered the changes. Were all men like that? Mad one minute and all smiles the next? She had vague memories of her father laughing as they ran around the yard long ago, but not enough to erase those of him lashing out unexpectedly with his calloused hand.

She was relieved by Matt's happy mood. She tried to tell herself maybe he had a right to be upset when he woke up and found her gone. How could he know she'd be back? Was that what love was—wanting someone there all the time, not letting them go away without saying good-bye or knowing when they'd be back? It was one of the nicest days they had. Matt wandered from one back road to another, heading east but not in any straight line. They went through a tiny town that had a Dairy Queen and stopped for malts and hamburgers. They parked off the road by a rushing brook where they sat in the shade of a quaking aspen and watched the water spilling over rocks in the afternoon sun. It was quiet except for the sound of the water and the birds singing in the trees. Kathy felt a contentment she'd never known. When Matt slipped his arm around her, she didn't pull away. They sat that way a long time, not talking, just being. Once Matt pointed to a silver flash as a fish darted through a small pool behind a rock.

117

Kathy leaned forward eagerly to watch it, then turned to Matt to share the wonder. His face was right next to hers. His arm seemed part of her as he drew her close and their lips touched. She shivered as he laid her back on the warm grass. She put her arms around his neck so he'd know she wanted him to stay. The kiss was different from the chaste, comforting one he'd given her the first night. She'd never kissed a boy before. Somehow she had the feeling Matt was as inexperienced as she was, but the kiss was the most wonderful thing she'd ever known. His lips were soft and moist, warm as though he were becoming part of her. Or maybe she was becoming part of him. Once she thought she felt the tip of his tongue touch hers, but she couldn't be sure. When he drew away, she smiled up at him without letting him go.

"That was nice."

He smiled. "You're my girl, Katie."

She didn't know why she got a funny feeling deep down inside when he said she was his girl. Maybe she wasn't quite ready for such a declaration. Or maybe because he hit her this morning.

Matt looked solemn. "I told your pa, we ain't done nuthin' bad, Katie, you know that."

She threaded her fingers into his ginger-colored hair and tugged gently, still smiling. Did she want more than a kiss? Her cheeks got warm and she looked at the canopy of branches over them. Matt was quiet a moment, then rolled to lie beside her, slipping his arm under her shoulders and drawing her head to his chest. His fingertips brushed her breast. She didn't pull away.

"Katie?"

"Um?"

"Would it really be bad?"

Was he asking her did she want to? How could she answer yes or no? But she'd asked herself the same question this morning and almost wished . . . "I don't know, Matt."

His fingertips moved hesitantly on her breast, gentle and

caressing, as if he wanted her to know it wasn't an accident. She had a funny trembling feeling, and she knew her nipples were poking up like they did when she got dressed on a cold morning. In a way, she felt cold but it was a delicious shivery chill that warmed her.

"Do you want to?" He spoke so softly, she wasn't sure the question wasn't inside her own head. She peeked at him. He was staring at the sky.

"I'm scared," she said. "I mean, I'd *be* scared." She was glad he didn't turn. She'd made it sound as if she was ready to do it.

"Yeah," he said very softly.

They fell silent, lost in the mystery of anticipation. After a long time, Matt said they had to go.

At dusk they stopped at a Chinese takeout place in Billings. Matt ordered recklessly and they left with two huge bags filled with steaming cartons. Giggling like kids, they asked directions to a nearby park. They found a table apart from the few picnickers enjoying the balmy evening. They emptied the bags, and Kathy tore one to make place mats for the picnic table that was splattered with bird droppings. Matt clowned and jabbered in pidgin English as he pulled his eyes up at the corners. Kathy couldn't remember ever having so much fun. By the time they finished eating, it was dark and mosquitoes buzzed relentlessly. Kathy gathered up the leftovers and put them in the empty bag. Matt took it from her and dropped it in the trash bin.

"There's enough food there for two more meals!" she protested.

"So? Tomorrow we're gonna eat in restaurants. No more picnics."

"Really?"

"Sure. We're gonna stay at one of those fancy hotels in Yellowstone and eat in the dining room."

"Matt!" She hugged him, smiling when he put his arms around her. She wanted him to kiss her again. Hesitantly, she raised her face. He bent to her lips. Standing there in the darkness, their bodies touching full length, Kathy's nipples tingled and hardened without his touching them. She was in awe of the wonderful new feelings her body encompassed. This time she was sure his tongue touched hers. She liked it.

"Let's get away from the mosquitoes," he said, swatting the air. He opened the van and they crawled in, pulling the door shut quickly. Kathy's heart pounded as Matt unrolled the sleeping bags. The silky sound sent shivers along her spine.

The moon was high enough to cast a pale glow. The other picnickers had gone; the park was quiet except for the crickets. Matt spread the sleeping bags carefully, then sat back on his heels.

"Katie?" It was a painful whisper.

She raised her arms and drew off the Grateful Dead T-shirt, dropped it, and reached back to unhook her bra. A shaft of moonlight bathed her. Her naked breasts looked like smooth marble as she let the bra fall. Matt made a low sound but didn't move. Slowly, Kathy drew down her jeans and underpants. They caught on her sneakers, and she pulled them all off together and pushed them aside in a tangled heap. She lay down on the sleeping bag.

Matt sat very still, breathing heavily through his mouth. Kathy shivered. Maybe he wasn't going to—maybe she . . .

He pulled off his shirt and unsnapped his jeans. He yanked off his tennis shoes without untying them, then snaked off the jeans and shorts. He was in the shadows so she couldn't see him clearly, but Kathy was excited, knowing he was naked. When he lay beside her, she pressed against him so her breasts and belly and hips touched his flesh. She felt the quick, hard pressure of his arousal and it intensified her own excitement. It was okay—it wasn't evil . . .

Hesitantly Matt raised himself over her. She spread her legs, then closed her eyes to savor the ecstasy of becoming a woman. *He loves me, so it's all right.* The air was cold on her overheated body as she felt the first pressure of Matt's penis touch the throbbing wetness between her legs. He pushed suddenly and she held her breath.

Matt began to hump roughly. She opened her eyes. There was nothing but his weight heavy on her. Experimentally, she twitched the muscles down there the way she did when she woke up at night with sensuous dreams. He wasn't in her at all. He was making believe. Didn't he know? Daringly, she reached down to guide him. Her hand closed around his limp organ. Matt pulled away and rolled aside.

After a long time she whispered, "Matt? It's okay. Really. I'm—I'm sort of glad we couldn't—you know. I was scared. Maybe we need time to think about it, you know? It was kind of sudden. Maybe we're not ready to take such a big step."

He sucked air into his lungs. "You sayin' you don't want to do it with me?"

"No, of course not. It's just—" Confusion swept her.

He rolled to face her but didn't touch her. "It'll be all right when we get to Yellowstone, you'll see. It'll be all right, won't it?" His voice was plaintive, and she wondered if he was crying.

"Sure, Matt," she said tenderly. "It'll be fine next time. When we get to Yellowstone it'll be perfect." She laid her hand on the pale blur of his cheek and touched his lips before she climbed into her sleeping bag.

22

Kay couldn't rouse herself. Her limbs were numb and her chest hurt as though the butcher knife had pierced her body as well as the old man's. When Matt finished pouring the gas, he ordered her to drive, but she couldn't move. Angrily he pulled her from behind the wheel and shook her.

"What's the matter with you! I said drive!"

Helpless, she sagged. He grabbed her before she fell.

"Katie? I didn't mean to hurt you. You okay? Say you're okay—"

He was so close she could smell the gasoline and blood. She forced herself to stand. "I'm—okay." She swallowed bile when she saw his blood-spattered shirt. She leaned against the car.

"Yeah, well, don't scare me like that, you hear?" He watched her, as though not quite sure.

Dear God, he killed a man . . . it's beginning again. . . .

"Katie?"

She fixed her gaze at a point beyond his shoulder. "The heat . . . I can't drive, Matt, please—" She broke into sobs and covered her face.

"Don't cry!" His tone was frightened and demanding.

Words stumbled out. "I don't feel good. Please don't make me drive."

"Okay, okay. Get in."

She staggered around the car, falling against the trunk

122

as the smell of spilled gasoline assailed her, averting her eyes from the pickup truck. She shuddered as she climbed in beside Jeff, who stared at her with a stricken expression. She pulled him onto her lap and buried her face in his hair.

Matt started the car and gunned it onto the road, tires screeching. Jeff whimpered, and Kay realized she was clutching him hard enough to hurt. She loosened her grip and breathed through her mouth as Matt glanced at her.

"You'll be okay when we get there," he said.

She nodded mutely. Slowly her mind was beginning to work again. They'd have to stop for gas. There couldn't have been more than a gallon or two in the can. Why had the old man lied? Her stomach churned dangerously as she remembered Matt's arm plunging down with the knife. *Stop it*, she told herself, *stop it!* Twenty-two miles to a gas station. Suppose someone found the pickup? Suppose the old man's wife went looking for him? In a rural community like this, everyone would know him. Minutes after he was discovered, the police—

She'd bolt when Matt stopped for gas. Make a run for it. The ladies' room! She'd lock herself in. She'd take Jeff and get inside before Matt could stop her. She hugged Jeff reassuringly. It would work. It had to.

Matt was driving fast, but she welcomed the reckless speed. The car pitched and jerked as she clung to Jeff. *No seat belts, not now.* When Matt looked at her, she forced a ghost of a smile. *Calm him down . . . let him think everything is all right.*

"I'm feeling better." Her voice came out a hoarse whisper. "If—if I could have a drink of water—" *Don't let him see how scared I am.*

Matt slowed as though relieved. Could she play on his concern? She experimented with ideas, rejecting anything dramatic. Just a drink of water, he'd understand that. It would be an excuse to go to the restroom.

Ten minutes down the road they passed a mailbox beside

a neatly painted fence. The old man's house. Kay looked away.

Endless road. Sheep grazing on a hillside. A tractor standing in a field. Another mailbox. Finally a stop sign where the road dead-ended into a wider highway. A green and white sign indicated a town in either direction. Matt drummed the steering wheel nervously, then turned toward Mack's Inn.

She saw the bright sign of the station after a few miles. When Matt didn't slow, she felt a stir of panic.

"Matt? There's a gas station. Can we stop?"

"We don't have time. We gotta get there."

"But we'll run out of gas again—" She choked down her fear.

He frowned, bringing his mind back from wherever it had been. He slowed, then spun the wheel sharply, cut into the drive, and pulled to a stop by the pumps. His face was filmed with sweat as he clutched the wheel. Kay had her hand on the door handle as her gaze searched the tiny station for a rest-room sign. She saw it inside the office as a man in coveralls came out of the garage wiping his hands on an oily rag.

"Howdy. Fill 'er up?"

Matt nodded, watching in the side mirror as the man uncapped the tank. Kay opened the door and slid out in a single motion, hugging Jeff. She heard the attendant's exclamation of surprise as she dashed past and flung herself inside. Behind her, she heard Matt's feet pound on the gravel. She threw herself against the door of the ladies' room, but Matt caught her before she could get inside. Blinded by panic, she kicked furiously and tried to pull away. A step—just a step—

With a wrench, Jeff was jerked out of her arms. Matt shoved her and sent her flying into the rest room. She turned like a snarling tigress, aware of the pain in her hip where it cracked against the washbasin, and grabbed for her strug-

gling son. But Matt was too quick. Stepping back, he pulled
the door shut. She tugged at the knob.

"Jeff! Matt—don't hurt him! I'm sorry, I'm sorry!" She
twisted the knob desperately, then fell against the door sobbing. "Matt, let me out. I'm sorry. Please—"

"Mommy—"

"Shut up, dummy."

Jeff's crying cut off abruptly. She pressed her face to the
grimy paint and forced down the clutching panic. "Please
let me out, Matt." She was a fool to think she could outwit
him. "Matt?"

His voice was strangely subdued. "Get your drink, Katie. We have to go."

She turned on the tap and splashed her face with tepid
water, then gulped some out of her hand. When she reached
for a paper towel, the gray face in the mirror was a wild-
eyed stranger. She heard a door slam and quickly tossed
away the towel.

"I'm done, Matt." Silence. "Matt?" She listened. Cautiously she turned the knob. The door gave. She opened it
slowly, peering out at the empty station. Where was Matt?
What had he done with Jeff? She heard a muffled sob from
the men's room and pushed the door open. Jeff was standing near the toilet, gulping sobs and shivering like a puppy.
She scooped him into her arms as her hands explored his
head and body. He was all right. He was all right!

With a start, she realized Matt was gone. Through the
grimy glass of the station, she saw the Toyota still at the
pump. Quickly, she slammed the door shut and slid the
bolt. Matt was gone. She and Jeff were safe. She put her
cheek on his and murmured soothing sounds as she tried
to listen. Surely the station attendant had seen what happened. Had he gone for help?

Jeff sobbed and she kissed his cheek, murmuring for him
to be quiet. Was that a noise outside? She put her ear to
the door.

"Katie?" It was so close she jumped back. "Open the door."

She pressed Jeff's face to her bosom and held her breath as the doorknob rattled. She glanced around the tiny room. There was no window, only a tiny air vent high on the wall. No weapon.

Something crashed against the door. She cowered in a corner. The second crash shook the door and jiggled the bolt. Why didn't the station man come?

The door splintered and flew inward as the bolt yanked loose. Matt filled the doorway, heaving for breath, his ginger hair spiking out like devil's horns. Kay's mouth opened but her scream died in a terrified moan as Matt came toward her in a slow-motion nightmare, air hissing between his teeth. His powerful hand swung, stinging her cheek and making her head ring. She couldn't escape the blows as she tried to protect Jeff. Her knees buckled and she felt herself sliding down the grimy wall. The roar in her head mingled with pain. She tasted salty blood as she sank into unconsciousness.

23

She drifted in a heavy fog, welcoming its embrace, not wanting to be let go. *Hold me . . . rock me . . . back and forth . . . gentle. Mama?* She wanted to sleep. *Rock me to sleep, Mama. . . . Love me. . . .* She let herself sink into the protective arms. *Now I lay me down to sleep. . . . Don't go away, Mama, please don't go away. . . .*

Mama? She fought the pull dragging her toward the surface. Her body ached. *Don't let Pa hit me—I'm a good girl, Mama. Why is Pa mad? I'll do whatever he says. Don't let him hit me, please, Mama. I'm a good girl, aren't I? Shh . . . good little girl. . . . Now I lay me down to sleep, I pray the Lord—does God love me, Mama?—my soul to keep. . . . Does Pa love me? If I should die before I wake—*

Something banged her shoulder and she opened her eyes. *Mama?* She blinked tear-swollen lids as she struggled with the nausea mushrooming in her throat. She was back in the car. The air was hot and stuffy, strangling her. Panicked as reality flooded back, she realized Jeff wasn't beside her. She twisted, then sobbed as she saw him curled on the back seat, his eyes closed, his thumb in his mouth. She slumped helplessly against the car door.

Matt's gaze turned to her. "You lied to me, Katie. You promised, but you were lying." His look was filled with accusation.

She remembered the gas station, the crashing door.

127

Aware of pain, she saw the huge discoloration on her arm and felt her swollen lip. It had all been for nothing. She'd made things worse. She eased her bruised shoulder from the door. He'd won, and now they were moving steadily closer to his destination.

She knew where they were going. No matter how she tried to delude herself that she was safe as long as they headed north, it wasn't true. He was taking her back, sucking her relentlessly into the nightmare from which she'd never escaped. Only, this time, he had Jeff too.

"Don't lie to me no more, Katie. When you make a promise, you gotta keep it. You always used to keep your promises. Not like my pa. Do you know the lake there is cold even in the summer? All those streams from the mountains when the snow melts. Real cold."

A chill began in her bones and spread outward. They were going back to Yellowstone.

24

Harriet insisted they have dinner at the hotel. "We'll save the cookout stuff until we need it. When was the last good meal you had?"

He let himself be led across to the majestic old hotel that glowed with bright lights. The sound of a piano hovered in the air with the faint mist of the hot springs.

"We won't have any trouble getting served at this hour," Harriet said. "We'll get back to Bass in plenty of time."

They sat at a table near the window in the elegant, high-ceilinged green and pink dining room that was a picture out of the past. A cool breeze came through the open window where moths fluttered against the screen. Elliot went along with Harriet's recommendation of the trout, which she said was excellent. He sipped his drink, which she also insisted he needed, and stared at the glittering limestone terraces illuminated by the lights on the access road.

"I know it's trite to say relax," Harriet said, "but you won't be any good to Kay and Jeff if you're exhausted. We're going to have to keep our wits about us every minute."

"I feel so damned helpless."

"I know, but we can't blunder around in the dark. Give Bass a chance, then we'll go from there."

"I've been wondering if Briggs will head for Bridge Bay or if there was something else he meant to do here, something he didn't get to after the murders. If only I could remember everything Kay told me!''

"Don't keep punishing yourself, Elliot. It's coming back in bits and pieces.''

"Not fast enough. Briggs is a killer. Suppose he—''

"Stop it, Elliot!'' Harriet set down her drink with a small thud.

He inhaled, letting his lungs absorb oxygen. "Sorry. You're right. I won't be worth a damn if I lose control. Show me that map so I can get an idea of distances and locations.''

Harriet shifted her glass and spread the map. With a fingertip, she pinpointed Mammoth, then traced the routes to the other areas of the park and campgrounds. For the first time, Elliot recognized the monumental task they'd undertaken. There were miles of roads and trails, with long, lonely stretches between. Bridge Bay was almost in the center of the park on the west side of Yellowstone Lake. Briggs could get to it from any direction.

When the food came, Harriet folded the map. "No worrying while we eat,'' she admonished gently, knowing it was like telling him not to breathe. She tried to distract him by talking about her last visit to the park with Wayne, but she knew she was only keeping Elliot's tongue quiet, not his mind. When they finally paid the check and left, he set a brisk pace for the ranger headquarters.

"There's no sign of them at Bridge Bay,'' Bass told them without preamble. "Every registration card matches a vehicle in the campground and the reservation list. The pictures are on the way to every gate, and today's crews from North and West came in to look at them. We didn't get a positive ID, but the girl who worked the West Gate this afternoon thinks the man's photo looks vaguely familiar.''

Elliot couldn't control his excitement, despite his dismay that Briggs might already be inside the park.

Bass said, "It's hard to make a positive identification

from this kind of picture. What stuck in Sally's mind was that the man didn't want to talk. She made some cheerful remark, but he didn't say a word. It happens sometimes, but usually someone in the car responds, if only to say thanks.''

"The woman and child . . . ?''

"She didn't get a good look at either of them. The gatehouses are above the level of the cars, so passengers aren't in a direct line of vision.''

"Does she remember the car?''

Bass shook his head. "She sees hundreds of cars a day.''

"Can we talk to her?'' Elliot asked. It was the first lead, no matter how faint, and Harriet guessed Briggs would use the west or south entrance.

"It won't do any good—'' Bass shrugged. "She lives in staff housing.'' He gave them directions to find the building. "I understand your anxiety, Mr. Pier, but I have to request that you stay here and leave this to my men. The rest of the reports will be in by morning, and we may have something concrete.''

Elliot held up his hand. "I can't sit around doing nothing. My wife and son are out there with a killer.''

"Then that request is an order,'' Bass said.

"Order what you damn please, but you can't stop me,'' Elliot snapped. He was sick of official wait-and-see tactics.

Bass regarded him uncertainly for several seconds. "All right. I won't try to stop you, but a word of warning: stay on the regular trails. Our biggest problem in the park is people who think it's okay to break the rules.'' He picked up a pen and wrote on a slip of paper, then handed it to Elliot. "My home phone number. I'll have calls routed there tonight. Reports should start coming in within two or three hours. Stay in touch.''

Sally Crane was a pert, honey blonde with an open smile and clear green eyes. "I wish I could be sure,'' she told Elliot and Harriet when she'd let them in. She perched on the edge of the bed after offering them the only chairs in the sparse room. She brushed back her long hair with an unconscious gesture. "That picture's pretty awful, you know?"

Harriet tried to put her at ease. "Mug shots aren't very flattering."

"I've never seen a convict before."

"Tell us everything you remember," Harriet encouraged.

Sally's head bobbed. "I told Mr. Bass I'm not sure, but the man looked a little like that. Kind of a long, thin face and those eyes. He looked mad at the world, you know?"

"What color was his hair?"

Sally frowned in concentration. "Brown, maybe a little reddish."

Elliot said, "Curly or straight?"

"Straight. It flopped over his forehead, I remember that. Not short but not real long. Sort of in between." She looked at them hopefully.

"What else did you notice?" Harriet coaxed.

"I only saw him for a few seconds. He had the money ready when he drove up. I handed him a ticket and map and told him to save the receipt to show if they wanted to get back in. That was it. Usually people have some kind of questions, but not him. He just drove through."

"What was he wearing? Jeans? Slacks? A sport shirt?"

"Gosh, I don't remember. I guess I didn't notice."

Harriet persisted. "Do you have an impression of color? Bright, dark, white?"

Sally flipped her hair back again. "Dark, maybe. I don't know for sure. The only reason I remember him at all was I didn't get any feeling of happiness, you know? People coming into the park on vacation are usually a little excited about it."

"Tell us about the boy," Elliot said.

"Well, he just sat there like a toy soldier, pressed against the seat like he was afraid to move. He had his thumb in his mouth. I thought at the time maybe his mom and dad had a fight or something. You know how kids get when that happens.''

Jeff sometimes resorted to his baby habit of thumb sucking when he was sick or upset. Elliot felt ill. ''You said he had blond hair. You're sure?''

She nodded. ''His head was down so that was all I really saw.''

''And the woman?''

''I didn't see her face.''

''Was she wearing jeans?''

''Yeah, blue jeans,'' Sally said, surprised by the recollection.

''What about her blouse or shirt?''

''The man was leaning forward. I only saw her legs.''

''Her shoes?''

Sally frowned. ''No, I'm sorry.''

''A purse maybe?'' Harriet said.

''I don't think so. Wait—maybe there was something on the floor. Yeah, there was something by her feet.''

''You're doing fine,'' Harriet said with a warm smile. ''Relax and try to see the picture again.''

Sally pursed her lips and closed her eyes. When she opened them, she said, ''It was a cloth pouch-type bag. I think it was khaki or tan.''

Elliot's pulse quickened. Kay always carried a huge purse that held Jeff's odds and ends as well as her own. He kidded her about them. She had a tan one with her when she drove him to the airport.

''Does that help?'' Sally asked hopefully.

''A great deal. We appreciate your help, Sally.'' Harriet gave her another smile.

''Gee, I hope you find them.'' She looked at Elliot with pain behind her green gaze. ''It must be awful for you.''

''Thanks,'' he said, meaning it. ''Can you think of anything at all about the car?''

She shook her head. ''I'm sorry. It wasn't important at

the time, you know? But I think it was a small car, not a big fancy one.''

They rose, and Sally jumped to her feet to walk them to the door.

''If you think of anything else, no matter how insignificant it seems, will you let Mr. Bass know right away?'' Elliot asked.

''Sure. Good luck.''

Outside, Elliot and Harriet walked toward the parking lot where they'd left the motor home.

''Kay had a canvas pouch bag,'' Harriet confirmed. ''It was the only one I saw her with the past two weeks.''

Elliot made a strangled sound. His brief elation was fading into gut fear. Briggs was already inside the park with Kay and Jeff. Where?

''A small car. It's not much to go on,'' Harriet said. ''If Sally's right, Kay and Jeff must be crazy with terror by now.''

His voice broke. ''I can't wait until morning, Harriet. I've got to do *something!*''

She put a comforting arm across his shoulder. ''Okay, let's go.''

25

Matt slowed the car as they approached the entrance to the park. His gaze swept nervously to the gatehouse where a girl in a park uniform leaned out to talk to the driver of the car ahead. Matt frowned, searching for an elusive memory. Then he reached into his pocket and brought out a handful of bills and dropped them in his lap. Without taking his eyes from the road, he picked up the knife and slipped it under his thigh before he rolled down the window.

Kay gripped her hands tightly in her lap. The knife was so close to Jeff, so threatening . . . Matt shot her a quick glance.

"You try anything and he gets it fast, no foolin' this time. Just keep your mouth shut, you hear?"

He pulled ahead slowly, reading the sign about entrance fees, then plucking a five-dollar bill from the money between his thighs. He held it out as he stopped at the gatehouse.

"Hi," the girl said with a smile. "Your ticket's good for two weeks. You can reenter the park as often as you want just by showing it." She handed him the ticket, a map, and his change. "Hope you have a wonderful stay. The weather's perfect for September. If you're planning on fishing, they say the trout are biting at—"

Matt already had the car moving. Beside him, Katie whimpered softly as she let out her breath. He smiled.

Maybe this time she'd keep her promise. She'd be happy now that they were here. He'd thought about it so long, he was all jumpy inside. Him and Katie. They were back.

The road wasn't crowded. Not like the other time. He didn't like crowds. He didn't like a lot of people butting into his business and asking stupid questions. He didn't want Katie talking to anyone but him. He felt warm thinking about the two of them walking along the lake in the moonlight. Just the two of them.

He glanced at her. Her hand was on the kid's knee. He'd forgotten about the kid. Why had he let Katie bring him along? No brat was going to spoil this trip. He didn't want a kid tagging along when him and Katie wanted to be alone. Maybe they'd go fishing. It had been a long time since he'd been fishing. He glanced at the kid, wondering if he knew how to fish. Naw, he was too little. *Littler than I was when Pa took me to the North Fork of the river that time.*

He remembered the warm sunshine on his face and how excited he was at going fishin' with Pa. Pa cast out the line and showed him how to hold the rod. He stood real quiet, like Pa told him, and waited. He waited a long time. He was good at waiting. Suddenly something pulled at the line and it began to reel out with a noise like a swarm of bees.

"Put your thumb on the stop! Jesus, Matt, can't you do anything right!" Pa grabbed the rod and pushed him so hard, Matt slipped on the muddy bank and fell. Cold wet soaked through his jeans. Pa was reeling in the fish, grinning and cussing as it broke the surface and glistened in the sunlight for a moment before it disappeared. It became a darting shadow in the water as it tried to get free. Matt watched, fascinated by the struggle between the dumb fish and the determined figure looming above him. Suddenly Matt hoped it got away. He didn't want Pa to reel it in. It was his fish. Pa had no right to take the rod away like that. He should tell him what to do, how to land the fish on his own.

With a splash, the fish leaped out of the water close to the bank. Matt reached for the line, but Pa kicked him aside with a muddy boot. "Stay outta my way, damn it!"

Matt battled tears as he watched the silvery gleam under the surface. It moved slower as Pa reeled steadily, drawing it close.

"Get the net, for crisake!"

Matt stared at the flopping fish. He could hear it panting, or was that the rush of the water?

"Goddam it, get the net!" Pa's boot flicked at Matt's hip. He jumped and tried to scramble up the bank but his sneakers skidded in the mud and he sprawled flat. Pa cursed steadily as Matt scurried on all fours, wallowing in the slime and unable to stop the tears as the stones hurt his hands and knees. When he got to dry grass, he scrambled to his feet and ran to where Pa had left his gear. He grabbed the net and raced back, shoving it at Pa. Pa reached for it, but Matt was holding it out net first. Pa juggled to get hold of the handle as he cussed Matt angrily. Just as he got the net, the fish gave a twisting leap. The hook came out of its mouth. It flopped on the bank, then slithered into the water before Pa could reach it.

Pa threw down the rod and swung the net at Matt, hitting him hard across the head. "Goddam stupid little bastard! Why didn't you bring the net when I told you? Fuckin' fish must have been a good three-pounder! Jesus, you are a stupid little sissy prick!"

When they got home, the fish got bigger every time Pa told the story. Matt hated Ma for laughing and saying Pa should have known better than to take a scrawny little seven-year-old—and a dumb one at that—along. What did he expect? The two of them emptied the whiskey bottle and were still laughing when Matt fell asleep alone in his room upstairs.

Matt jerked the steering wheel as he remembered the hate and the pain. He wasn't going to take any stupid little kid fishing, that was for sure.

His head ached. Had to find a place to rest. Not while it was still light. Not when Katie might take a notion to run away again. But she wouldn't do that. He'd shown her. She knew better now. Anyhow, she loved him. This time she'd keep her promise. He rubbed his temple and tried to think. Dark soon. When it was dark, she wouldn't run away. Katie was scared of the dark. He smiled. He liked the dark.

A car passed them and he almost went off the road. He twisted the wheel, sweating. Got to pay attention, he told himself. We'll be there soon. We're in the park. The park.

He glanced at the towering trees closing in on the road. The sun was already in back of them. It was getting dark fast. How much farther did he have to drive? He tried to recall the detailed map he'd studied so often, but it was fuzzy in his mind. Did he turn soon? Was the road marked? He licked his lips as he tried to remember all the little things Juhnny had told him and the plan he'd worked out so carefully all by himself. He knew, it was just that he was tired. He wished he could ask Katie to read the map for him, but he didn't want anyone touching it, not even Katie. It was his. Juhnny had given it to him. It was his. Like the fish.

A motor home passed going the other way. He turned to watch it. It was a big one, like—Katie's gasp made him look back quickly as the car veered onto the shoulder. Angrily, he brought it back where it belonged. He shot a glance at the rear-view mirror but the motor home was already out of sight. Another car went by, then one pulling a trailer. Too much traffic. He didn't like traffic. It scared him because he had to be careful he wasn't sucked into the gulping rush of air as they passed. Where were they all coming from all of a sudden? He was sweating again.

He came to a junction and slowed to read the signs. It was hard to see all the names and arrows even though he was barely moving. Then suddenly they were in a busy place. Buildings . . . cars . . . people . . . men in uniforms. Noise filled his head. His hands jerked on the wheel. Not cops. Rangers. He didn't like rangers. He didn't like anyone in uniform. Except maybe the girl back there at the gate. She was pretty. He should have smiled at her. He put on the brake. Shit. He'd driven into a parking lot. He missed the turn. He had to go back. He clenched the wheel. His palms were wet and his legs were trembling. *Think! Get it right this time.*

He circled the lot at a crawl and put one hand on the knife, just in case. Two teenagers crossed right in front of him, not paying attention to where they were going. Laughing as if he didn't have a right to be there. He saw Katie move, and he drew out the knife so she'd see it. She sat back.

There was another sign at the end of the parking lot. This time he stopped, not caring about the car behind him, and read the sign slowly. Norris. That was it. He had to go through Norris. The map was clear as day inside his head now. Through Norris and Canyon, then down to the lake. He smiled. There was a park center at Canyon, with campgrounds and a restaurant and cabins. He remembered it all. From there it was less than an hour to the lake. He had plenty of time.

Kay hadn't been able to subdue the nausea that churned her stomach since they'd entered the park. She was still numb from Matt's blows, but seeing the park entrance had roused her from her stupor. Now terror dragged her toward the abyss of a nightmare past. She struggled against it, forcing herself to think about Jeff. He needed her. She couldn't let Matt hit him anymore. For a moment in the parking lot, her hope soared, but no one paid the slightest attention to the car or the people in it. She pressed her tongue against her swollen lip until the pain overrode her self-pity.

The shadows lengthened quickly, and night claimed the sky. Matt drove through Norris and turned on the road toward Canyon. Kay was shivering despite the sweater.

Should she remember these names? Had they been here before? Her brain bogged. For eleven years she had done everything she could to wipe out those memories. Now, when she tried to call them forth, they were mired deep behind the wall she'd built.

At Canyon, Matt slowed. The headlights picked out half a dozen signs, but the words blurred in Kay's vision. Matt waited for a car to go past on the intersecting road, then drove straight ahead. Kay saw the lights of a gas station. Beyond a screen of trees, lots of lights. A sign pointed toward the Visitor Center. Matt turned in. It was no mistake this time. He'd read the signs carefully, she was sure. She held her breath as he drove into the huge parking lot. Stores, restaurants, cabins . . .

The parking lot was filled and lights blazed. People strolled by store windows, and there was a steady flow in and out of the restaurants. Behind the plate-glass window of an ice cream parlor, Kay saw teenagers laughing and talking. If Matt took them into any of these places, she and Jeff would have a chance . . .

The knife. She glanced at the handle sticking out under Matt's leg. Cautiously, she moved her hand. Her heart stopped as Matt looked at her. The eerie light made his features grotesque; his eyes gleamed as he shoved the knife out of sight. *He can read my thoughts.* She looked away.

When he completed a slow circle of the parking lot, Matt turned in the direction of the campground. Kay was shaking so hard her bones seemed to rattle against her bruises, blanketing her with pain. It was hard to think beyond the pain. Campground. She didn't want to think. If he went into the campground, she wouldn't be able to choke off the scream that was gathering in her throat.

Matt drove past the campground entrance slowly. Among the trees, lights twinkled like distant stars. When they didn't turn in, Kay collapsed with relief. She felt Jeff's weight against her and knew he was asleep. Thank God.

Another road sign came into the beam of the headlights

but she saw it too late to read anything but ONE WAY. It was deserted except for the Toyota. The woods were so close, the road seemed like a tunnel. She shivered. Her throat was raw and her cheeks felt flushed. She clenched her hands when Matt turned off on a narrow trail.

"Oh, God, no—" She realized the peculiar sound that filled the car was her sobbing.

Matt stopped, shut off the engine, and took the keys as he got out. Kay bit her knuckle. He was going to leave her here—She heard the trunk open, then suddenly her door, and he was beside her. When he reached for her, she shrank away.

"Get out, Katie."

"No—I can't—"

He dragged her out. Jeff fell sideways across the seat as Matt scooped Kay in his arms. He carried her to the back of the car, pinning her arms when she tried to struggle.

"Don't—for God's sake, Matt—don't—"

"Shut up!"

She screwed her eyes tight against her panic. He couldn't leave her here . . . He was putting her down. He was going to leave her alone in the woods . . . Something hard and cold pressed at her back, and she tried to get up. Matt pushed her down.

"I can't trust you, Katie. Now you wait for me, promise?" He laughed as the trunk lid slammed on Kay's terrified scream.

26

In the morning Matt was as chipper as the squirrels search-ing for scraps under the picnic table. He insisted on an early start because they were going to Yellowstone. He talked excitedly, laughing and planning. His pa had prom-ised long ago to take him camping in Yellowstone but, like most of his father's promises, it had never happened. Matt wasn't mad like he usually was when he talked about his father's broken promises. He'd take her instead, he told her. She'd like Yellowstone. He read about it in an ency-clopedia. Someday he was going to read a whole book about it. If he'd known they were coming, he'd have done it already. "Just wait and see how great it is, Katie. I'll tell you all about it."

"Are there a lot of hotels?"

"Only a few. Did you know Teddy Roosevelt used to hunt bears in Yellowstone?"

"Teddy Roosevelt?"

"They didn't have roads and stuff then. They went everywhere on horses."

"But they have hotels now," she said, watching him. "And we're going to stay in one, right?"

"Sure. There's one right by the—that thing that spouts up."

"Old Faithful."

142

"Yeah. Did you know they can tell when it's going to go off? They got a way to figure it out."

"Maybe we'll be able to watch it from our room."

"Teddy Roosevelt stayed in a tent."

She glanced at him suspiciously, wondering if he was trying to get out of his promise.

"That was before they built the hotels. Old Faithful Hotel. Yeah. That's where we're gonna stay." He grinned, and Kathy giggled with excitement. She'd never stayed in a hotel. How big would it be? Bigger than the Frontier on Main Street, she'd bet. Bigger than anything in Blue Canyon probably. Or maybe even John Day or Burns. Maybe bigger than anything in Bend, but she couldn't be sure about that because she'd never been to Bend, only seen pictures in the *Oregonian*. But she knew *hotels* had maid service. She wouldn't make a mistake about the bed again.

"What's so funny?" Matt asked.

She realized she was smiling. "Oh, I was just thinking."

"About what?"

"Staying in the hotel and everything. It's going to be like a honeymoon," she said, then blushed.

They didn't get to Yellowstone until evening. For all his excited talk, Matt dallied along the road and made a big deal about their "last" picnic lunch, eaten alongside a rushing river they'd had to climb down a steep bank to reach. He talked endlessly about Yellowstone, repeating himself when he ran out of new information. A couple of times she almost asked him why they didn't just get there if he was so anxious, but she didn't want to risk spoiling his mood.

Now it would be dark soon. There were already long shadows across the road and she couldn't see the sun anymore. She wondered how far it was to the hotel.

They stopped at a gate where a cute guy in a neat uniform said they had to pay to get in. When Matt paid, the man gave them a map of the park. There was hardly enough light to see, but Kathy squinted at it until she found Old Faithful. And right there on the map it said: Old Faithful Inn.

"I wish we had a radio. I feel like music." She snapped her fingers to an imaginary beat, swaying and grinning. "Do you like music, Matt?"

"Sure."

"Maybe we can go dancing. Are you a good dancer? I practice in my room, but Pa won't let me—"

Matt's head jerked around. "Your pa ain't got nuthin' to say no more, you hear! Stop talking about him all the time. You want to dance, you can dance."

She recoiled. She hadn't meant . . . Boy, he was as bad as her father, jumping all over her like that. She hadn't been away from home all that long that she could remember never to even *mention* Pa. She found herself apologizing automatically, in spite of being mad.

"I'm sorry Matt. I didn't mean anything."

"Yeah, well, I'm sick of hearing about your pa. Forget him. He don't want you anymore. Only me. I want you, Katie. I'll always want you."

Somehow the mood was spoiled. "Sure, Matt." She tried to think about the hotel again and recapture her excitement, but it was gone like the light. There one minute, vanished the next. Matt put on the headlights, but they barely picked out the road between the dark woods on either side. Kathy folded her arms across her breasts. The park was spooky in the dark. She didn't like it. It would be okay when they got to the hotel. Lights, people, warm.

All of a sudden Matt slowed and turned onto a road she hadn't noticed. The van bounced and swayed. In the glare of the headlights she saw an unpaved, rough dirt trail.

"Where are we going?" she demanded. A big hotel would have a better road than this. The woods closed around them like a fist. Her chest felt like it did when she woke up at night with the covers all tangled around her so she couldn't breathe. She grabbed Matt's arm. "Where are we going?"

He pulled away. "I just want to see where this goes."

"But you promised—"

"I didn't promise! I said maybe."

"You did too!"

"I didn't! I know what I said! Now shut up so I can drive."

She withdrew sulkily. He *had* promised. He'd said they'd stay at the Old Faithful Inn. He said for sure. What right did he have getting mad and yelling because she believed him?

A branch scraped the van and she jumped. The woods were so dark. It was as if there never had been any light. Just pitch-blackness, like the bottom of a deep hole, except for the headlights. If he turned them off . . . She hugged her arms across her chest. Matt wouldn't stop here. There was nothing in the woods, except maybe wild animals. All that talk about Teddy Roosevelt and bears . . . Her fists were clenched so tight her nails dug into her palms. She watched Matt hunch over the wheel, peering ahead. He didn't know where they were! He'd made one of his stupid turns without any reason. Suppose there wasn't any way out? Suppose they got stuck? Suppose they had to stay until someone found them—all night . . . She hugged her arms.

The road goes somewhere. Every road has to go somewhere. Don't think about the woods. Teddy Roosevelt stayed here in a tent, and nothing happened to him. I wish I had a radio. Music. Don't think about the dark. She stared down at her hands. Don't look out. There'll be lights soon. And people.

The van bumped in a rut. There was a harsh scraping noise, then a heavy whack. Matt's breath hissed as he tried to get the van back under control. The headlight beams fanned the woods. Trees blurred in a curtain of green. A huge pine was detailed momentarily before the van hit it.

Kathy flung up her hands as she pitched forward. She screamed and buried her face in her arm, sobbing.

"Shut up!" Matt yelled.

She hiccuped, realizing she wasn't hurt, only scared. The van had stalled, and Matt was trying to start it. A whining metallic sound pierced the stillness. When it stopped, Kathy peeked through her fingers. Matt was staring at her. She sat up.

"It's your fault," he said furiously. "You grabbed me!"

"You're crazy—" Her lip trembled.

"Guess we'll just have to stay here."

Her anger vanished in a surge of terror. "No—please, Matt. You said we'd stay at the hotel. The van will start. It's just flooded. Let it sit a minute, then it'll start. Pa says—"

He hit her so fast and hard, she fell against the dash. Matt's fingers dug into her shoulder and pulled her back. "Quit talking about your pa! You got no one but me!"

She cringed and put her hand to her jaw. He had no right to hit her. She wasn't going to stay with him if he kept hitting her like that. If you loved someone, you didn't go around hitting them for no reason. She was shaking all over now. She wouldn't stay with him if he hit her. But where was she going to go? She glanced nervously at the dark woods.

If he left the headlights on, the battery would run down. They'd never get the van started. Beyond the shaft of light, spooky shadows moved stealthily. A whimpering sound came out before she could stop it. The headlights were getting dimmer already, she was sure. The shadows were darker. There—that one moved! It was coming closer!

She wrung her hands. "Matt, please try it again. It'll start, I know it will—"

He hit her again, but this time she didn't feel it.

"The battery's running down! We've got to get out of here!"

He grabbed her hair and pulled her face close. "Don't give me orders! It's all your fault."

She was beyond fear of his fury. "Please, Matt. I'll do anything. I'm so scared—"

His frozen gaze imprisoned her like a bubble in a block of ice as the darkness whispered around the van.

"Nothing to be scared of," he said, letting go of her. "I won't let nothin' happen to you." Smiling, he turned back to the wheel.

She wanted to tell him to turn off the headlights until he got it started, but she was too terrified of the darkness that would engulf them. She pressed her lips between her teeth as he turned the ignition. It ground, almost caught, ground again.

Not too much gas—don't flood it!

It whined, then caught. Matt laughed as though he'd done something clever. When he looked at her, she tried to smile. Slowly, Matt backed the van out of the tangled brush to the road. Carefully, he turned around and headed back the way they'd come.

27

As they walked back to the motor home, Elliot considered the odds of their quest. A needle in a haystack. Worse. If Briggs changed cars again, the odds were even more in his favor unless he left some trail. *Trail of blood . . . Jesus— Don't even think about it.* The darkness was getting to him. Kay hated the dark. It had taken a lot of gentling to get her to go outside at night. Here with Briggs, she'd be a basket case. But she and Jeff were alive. He clung to that. If Briggs had brought them this far, he wouldn't kill them now, would he?

In the motor home, they studied the park map again, weighing the routes to Bridge Bay. Harriet eliminated the road through Tower Junction. It was steep and winding, and if Briggs had come in the west entrance it would be his least likely choice. "Besides," she observed, "the campgrounds on that road are for tents only. There isn't much chance Briggs has that kind of gear."

The possibility of Briggs making a rough camp hadn't occurred to Elliot, and the idea wasn't pleasant. But Harriet was right, it wasn't logical, even for someone as illogical as Briggs.

They decided to take the shortest route to Bridge Bay and briefly considered checking out the campgrounds en route but decided against it. There wasn't much they could do prowling around campsites in the dark. Harriet offered to drive, but Elliot felt better with something to occupy his hands.

It was almost midnight when they reached Bridge Bay. Behind them, moonlight glazed the surface of Yellowstone Lake to a cold, gray sheet. The marina was hidden in a dark pocket beyond the campground entrance and a parking lot. Elliot pulled in behind the single spotlight that glared from the corner of a building. He sat staring at the dark shapes of boats moored at the jutting docks. With a sudden flash of memory, Kay's description made him feel as if he'd been here before. Elliot glanced back to where the campground was shrouded in darkness except for a light blinking faintly through the trees.

He stared at it. *They stopped somewhere else first, some service road where Kay panicked when Briggs got stuck. Then they came to the campgrounds. Parked by the light. Rest rooms and showers.* Fragments were sliding together. Elliot felt a tingle of excitement. It was coming back gradually, jogged by being in the places Kay had described.

"I'm going to walk through the campgrounds," he said.

"What good—" Harriet stopped when she saw the expression on his face. "Okay. We'd better put on jackets. It's gotten cold."

The campground lay like an outstretched hand in the woods, curled fingers reaching into the darkness. The office at the mouth of the service road was closed. Elliot beamed the flashlight on the bulletin board. As he read the notice that gave instructions for using sites after hours, another bit of memory fitted into place. *The Dodge woman offered to help fill out the registration.* There was also a warning that bears were known to frequent the area; no soft-sided camping equipment was permitted.

The light was on a central building of the first looping finger of campsites. Its glow faintly illuminated parked campers, trailers, and motor homes. There were only a few cars, big ones capable of hauling heavy loads. No compacts. There was one van. Sweat beaded under the collar of Elliot's jacket. Briggs had a van the first time. Nervously, Elliot wiped his mouth.

Suddenly a light came on in a camper two sites down. A man carrying a flashlight stepped out, easing the door shut behind him. He came up short as he saw Elliot and Harriet in the road.

"Howdy, friends," he said in a low voice. "You gave me a start. I thought I was the only one with weak kidneys." He chuckled.

"Sorry," Elliot whispered, then improvised quickly. "We're looking for friends we're supposed to meet. We got our signals crossed. Do you happen to know if a young couple with a little blond-haired boy came in today?"

The man scratched the stubble on his chin. "Don't think so. Of course, I don't know everyone down the end of the line."

"Have you been here most of the day?"

"All day," he said. "We got in yesterday about noon and nothing would do but we take the boat tour right off. Then my wife wanted to hike up to Lake and Fishing Bridge. No matter I'd been driving five hundred miles. So this morning I put my foot down. My day off. I didn't budge past the boat ramp."

"Would you have seen everyone who checked in?"

The man cocked his head. "You're mighty curious, friend."

Harriet said disarmingly, "We don't mean to be. It's just that we'd really like to find our friends tonight."

"Some kind of trouble?" the man asked curiously.

"A family emergency," Elliot said.

The man rubbed his chin again. "Well, like I said, I'm pretty sure there's no one here like you described. Matter of fact, no kids at all I know of in this loop."

"Thanks," Harriet whispered, slipping her arm through Elliot's and turning him back toward the marina. "Have a nice vacation."

"You too," he called after them. "If your friends come

by, I'll tell them you're looking for them. Could be they got delayed driving. Happens.''

"Thank you. Good night," Harriet whispered over her shoulder. When they were out of earshot, she said, "We're going to be in trouble if we have people eager to tell Briggs we're looking for him."

She was right. Elliot was suddenly very tired as they walked back to the motor home.

28

The darkness kept the eyes from watching him. In the dark, Matt was better than any of them. He could see clearly and know what people were really like. Inside. He could see right inside them. He knew what they felt and what they were thinking. Like watching a fish in a clear stream. The fish didn't like being caught. He knew that as soon as Pa pulled it out of the water. It hurt, and Matt felt the pain. Pa shouldn't have done that to his fish. It was his fish. Pa had no right.

He stopped and stood in the deep shadows near the entrance to the parking lot. It was quieter now. Like Katie. He didn't like locking her in the trunk that way, but she had to learn to keep her promises. It was that stupid kid. Sometimes Katie thought more about the kid than she did her promises. Should have put him in the woods for the bears instead of leaving him in the car. Stupid little sissy prick. Should have known better than to bring him.

One restaurant was still open, and there were plenty of cars and campers in the lot. He walked among them slowly. When the door of the restaurant opened, he heard voices. He stopped as four people came toward him. He ducked behind a van until they passed. At the far end of the row, they climbed into a car and drove off.

The metal of the van was cool under his hand. He tried the door, but it was locked. It didn't matter. Katie didn't like vans. She wanted a motor home, like that talky woman and her husband—what was their name? He didn't remember. Sometimes he remembered everything so clear it was like pictures were painted inside his skull. But other times, no matter how hard he tried, it was all gray and dim, like the walls of his cell. He remembered Katie that night with the lamplight soft on her hair as she listened to the radio. He hadn't liked the radio either, but he didn't remember why. Maybe Katie wanted to listen to it instead of being with him. That would make him mad.

He picked his way along the row of parked vehicles. There it was. He quickened his step, circling the motor home critically. Yup, he decided, Katie would like it. It was smaller than what's-their-names', but it was shiny and new. He jiggled the door handle, but it didn't give. He squatted in the shadows to wait. He was good at waiting.

The sound of voices roused him. He eased up and glanced toward the restaurant. Some people had come out and were standing near the door. After a few minutes they split up, saying good-bye loud enough for him to hear. When one couple headed toward him, he melted into the shadows.

At the motor home, the man put a key in the lock. Matt stepped behind him silently. The woman gave a startled little cry and put her hand to her chest. The man started to turn, but Matt grabbed him, jerking his head back so the guy's skinny neck was stretched tight. Matt drew the knife blade hard across the pale skin with a quick motion. The woman's mouth worked like a fish's, but only funny muffled noises came out. Matt let the old man slump and lunged at her. She began to fall before the knife touched her, still clutching her chest, her eyes bulging. Matt yanked her hand away and plunged the blade into her chest. When she was still, he straightened and looked around. At the far end of the lot, a car started. Its backup lights gleamed like cats' eyes. Matt ducked as the headlights fanned past. When the taillights disappeared at the end of the lot, he rolled the two bodies under the high frame of a pickup parked next to the motor home.

Using the keys the man had left in the lock, he got in and sat behind the wheel. He had to squint at the dashboard, but he found the ignition and got the engine started. As he turned on the headlights, a car pulled out behind him somewhere. Matt waited for the sound to fade in the distance before he backed the motor home out carefully so he wouldn't hit anything. In the sweep of the headlights, a slow trickle of blood ran like black ink from under the pickup.

29

Elliot crawled into the bed that folded down across the out-of-use table, but sleep didn't come. He tried all the gimmicks that occasionally worked: deep, regular breathing, letting his body relax in stages, clearing his mind systematically. But each time he ventured close to the edge of unconsciousness the thought of Kay and Jeff snapped him back cruelly. They were out there with a madman. And inside Elliot's head a piece of the puzzle stubbornly refused to slip in place. It was close, but it hovered on the outskirts of his memory waiting for the right signal to call it in. The clue he needed. Damn. He and Kay had worked six years to rid her of painful memories that didn't want to be erased. Now when he needed them they refused to cast so much as a ghost image in his mind.

He stared out into the night. Shadows took on a third dimension as a breeze rustled the trees in the pale moonlight. Kay . . . Kathy . . . When she got out of Frontera, she didn't want to be called Kathy anymore. Kathy was a child of the past. She wanted to start a new life and forget the past. Kay was the new woman. At first she'd been shy, like a wistful child playing at grownup. Los Angeles was an awesome, fantasy Emerald City. Over tostadas at El Coyote, she told him it was like a dream that she was afraid would disappear when she opened her eyes. As a kid in Oregon and during her five years in prison, she tried to envision herself in a city like Los Angeles. Her mind conjured streets and cars and stores, but the reality took her breath away. The steady intensity of the traffic astonished her, and the noise was overwhelming. So different from the sounds of the lumber mill in Blue Canyon or the heavy clank of steel gates in prison. Her imagination had been unable to conceive what was totally beyond her experience. Imagined noise didn't get louder or softer, and it wasn't in the background every waking moment the way the sound of Los Angeles was, rising and falling like the drone of bees around a hive. She especially loved the city lights. She liked never being in total darkness, even in the middle of the night. She insisted on keeping the curtains open so, if she woke, the blinking lights were always there below the hill.

Now she was out there in the dark. Elliot's heart wrenched. *I love you, Kay . . . and goddam it, I'll find you! I'm coming for you, darling—*

He closed his eyes and tried to focus on relaxing. *Pick a single thought,* he told himself. *A sound. Insects chirping . . . the soft lap of water against the shore. . . .*

He sat up abruptly, his face close to the window. Water. Something about water—the sound of it . . . A waterfall! There had been a waterfall where Briggs parked the van and left Kathy alone that night!

Quietly, he slipped from bed and found the park map. Unfolding it, he snapped on the flashlight, shielding the beam so he wouldn't disturb Harriet. He located Bridge Bay and studied the area. There were probably hundreds of waterfalls in the park, but the one he was looking for had to be within walking distance. He traced circles with his fingertip, peering at the tiny identifying inscriptions: Bridge Bay, Gull Point Drive, Natural Bridge. He stopped and read it again: Natural Bridge. That could be it. Bridges usually meant water, maybe a waterfall. There could be waterfalls in any of the dozens of streams and rivers that crisscrossed the park. Half of them probably weren't even on the map. But Kay had described the spot as lonely, so it probably wasn't a major scenic attraction. It didn't even have to be much of a waterfall. It might have been a tiny shelf in a stream bed, magnified by Kay's fear.

Natural Bridge. Could he find it in the dark? He measured the distance with his thumb, checking it against the scale. Couple of miles at most. But the road would be dark in the woods. And the beam of a flashlight could easily be seen a long way off.

Wait for dawn, he told himself. And then what? For the first time he wished he had a gun.

30

The wind numbed her. Each breath drew the cold deeper into her bones. She tried to make her feet keep moving, but they were too heavy. Crying, she sat down on the brittle, frosty grass and closed her eyes. *If I should die before I wake* . . .

"Get up, Kathy. Come on, honey."

"I can't, Mama. I'm so tired."

"Just a little way more, baby, please. For me?"

The tears turned icy on Kathy's cheeks. She could still hear Pa shouting and Mama crying as he hit her, and the door slamming as Pa stormed out to the pickup and drove away. Mama had put some clothes in a suitcase, bundled Kathy into her heavy coat, then taken the egg money from the pitcher on the mantel before they left. But they'd walked so far. Even though they weren't to town yet, Kathy thought she'd never been so far from home. She looked up at Mama.

"Where will we go?" she asked plaintively. She didn't want to go back to Pa, but it was so cold . . .

There were tears in Mama's eyes as she knelt and took Kathy in her arms. For a long time there was only the sound of winter slicing through the pines. Mama's damp cheek nuzzled Kathy's.

"Oh, Kathy, baby—" Mama rocked her gently. After a while she struggled to her feet, lifting Kathy and holding her tight so she wouldn't sink back to the frozen ground.

The wind made a strange sobbing sound, or maybe it was Mama.

"Baby, baby—"

I'm not a baby, I'm a big girl. Too big to carry. She pressed her face into Mama's coat and tried so hard not to cry. Mama's voice came from a long way off, sighing like the wind.

"All right, honey, we'll go back . . . we'll go home."

If I should die before I wake . . .

She felt Jeff's warm body pressed against her and opened her eyes. The persistent, low rumbling inside her head made it difficult to think, to remember. Jeff was here, safe. Did anything else matter? She let herself drift in the warm cocoon, not cold anymore. They were going home. She didn't remember Elliot coming for them, but he was taking them home. She burrowed in the comforting warmth. Elliot was taking them home. She closed her eyes.

"I won't wear it . . . I can't—don't make me!"

"Red is your favorite color, Katie."

Blood red . . .

"Your pa's dead. You can't ever go back."

Pa's blood. Blood red . . .

Cold moonlight bathed her and she shivered. "Put the sweater on, Katie. Don't make me mad." "Mama, where are we going?" "Shhh, shhh, we're going back." "Elliot? Where are you going?" He looked back before he walked away in the cold moonlight and disappeared in the shadows. Elliot?

If I should die before I wake . . .

31

Elliot scribbled a note for Harriet and taped it to the door. Then, picking up his jacket and the flashlight, he let himself out and stood a moment to orient himself in the crisp night. The floodlight cast dancing shadows across the water, which lapped against the shoreline like a lullaby. He headed toward the road.

At the entrance to the campground he glanced at the light winking through the trees. Briggs wouldn't pull into a well-habited area. He'd head for isolation. The loner.

A gibbous moon splashed coldly across the lake. It was bright enough so he didn't have to use the flash as he walked along the small stretch of highway that would take him to the thin line of a road marked on the map. After he crossed the bridge spanning the marina outlet he began looking for a sign. The wind had calmed to a chilly breeze, and he zipped his jacket. When he saw the outline of a sign, he snapped on the flashlight for a moment to read it. NATURAL BRIDGE.

The dirt road was narrow and rutted. A few yards into the woods, he had to turn on the flash as the forest closed around the road, trying to claim back what had been part of it. Centuries-old pines barred the moonlight except for a patch here and there. How far was it safe to use the light? A mile maybe, no more. He kept the beam trained on the ground so it was a small wobbly circle and counted his

160

steps echoing in the quiet. The darkness magnified every sound, though he knew he was moving almost silently.

Suppose a car was parked by the falls? What could he do? The futility of the night walk struck him. Startled, Briggs might kill Kay or Jeff before Elliot could break into the car. The sweat cooled on Elliot's face. He couldn't do a damn thing out here alone in the night like the wimpy heroine of a Gothic novel. He needed help. Harriet was right. Still, he didn't turn around.

He lost track of distance. To be on the safe side, he turned off the light and slowed. When he skidded on some loose rock he cursed silently but kept going. Briggs was a psycho. Dangerous. Ten years in prison hadn't changed that.

How far had he come from the highway? It couldn't be much farther. He slowed, testing each step like a cautious tiger. *Tiger.* Jeff.

Suddenly, instead of firm, hard ground, his shoes whispered on grass. He halted, confused, then crouched and put out his hand like a blind man. Rough, dewy grass. He moved his arm in a slow arc, pausing to feel a spiky bush directly in front of him. He was pretty sure he'd been walking in a straight line. If he hadn't changed course, the road had. Carefully, he backed up until he felt the solid road under his shoes. Crouching again, he examined it with broad sweeps, trying to readjust his eyes to the darkness.

The map showed a loop at the end of the road, a deadend turnaround at Natural Bridge. He cocked his head as he became aware of a faint sound. A gentle thrumming, barely discernible. A stream? A small or distant waterfall? His skin prickled. He couldn't pinpoint the sound. It was just out there, somewhere ahead of him.

He took several cautious steps to his left. The road began to climb. On his hands and knees he examined its width and followed it a few feet. Then he moved back to his starting position and did the same in the other direction. The angle of the right fork was lower, almost level. He moved along it slowly and was rewarded after a few yards by a patch of moonlight breaking through the trees. He stopped, breathing softly.

The sound of water was louder, and the woods thinned so fragments of moonlight dotted through. The road was a faint ribbon with dark borders. He studied the dark, blotchy shadows. Were they darker on the right? A cutback? Another road? He closed his eyes momentarily to erase the images, then looked again. There was a tiny flash of silver—a waterfall. Not a rushing cataract but a gentle free-falling stream against rocks. The one Kay had heard—

"At first I thought it was an animal outside the van. I was too scared to look. I lay there crying. There wasn't anything but dark woods all around, and there was nowhere to go."

Not a regular parking area. Briggs had pulled off the side of the road. Elliot searched the shadows methodically. No matter how hard he tried to give them form, there was no vehicle of any kind parked in the loop. He eased forward, skirting the patch of moonlight. He had to be sure.

At the faint sound of a twig snapping, Elliot froze. He listened for several moments, but there was only the wind soughing in the pines and the faint, delicate music of the waterfall. He went on. Before long the road began to rise and curve back on itself. Nothing. Not a goddam thing. He wasn't sure if he was relieved or angry. Wearily, he began retracing his steps.

32

The lake was frozen in the light of a half-moon caught on the ridge of mountains. Kathy hugged herself as she huddled on the cold seat. He'd scared her badly. She wondered if that was what he meant to do all along: promise to take her to a hotel, then drive her deep into the woods and frighten her half to death. All that talk about Teddy Roosevelt and bears. She shivered, wishing she had a sweater. The sweat shirt didn't keep her warm enough anymore.

Well, she wasn't going to say anything about the hotel, not after Matt's last outburst. She was still sore where he hit her. And she was still mad, but not as much as she was scared. Scared of the dark, eerie park. Scared of Matt. She wanted to go home. No matter what Pa said, she wanted to sleep in her own bed. She blinked furiously so she wouldn't cry.

Matt slowed, and she saw the sign in the headlights: BAY BRIDGE, MARINA, CAMPGROUNDS. He turned in. "They got nice campgrounds here. People come with trailers and stay a week sometimes."

No hotel. He really believed he had never promised. Nothing she said would change his mind now. With relief, she saw lights ahead, but it was only a parking lot. Matt drove around it slowly, then headed back the way they'd come. A little way down the road, he made another turn. She'd missed the sign before. Campgrounds. Well, it was better than the woods. Anything was better than the woods.

She was surprised how big it was. Lights twinkled among the trees, and she could hear voices and laughter. She sat up as Matt drove slowly along a road lined with campers, trailers, and motor homes. At some, people sat in lawn chairs or at picnic tables. One was set with a red-checked tablecloth with a glowing lantern on it. A woman was clearing away dirty dishes. Kathy wondered who was clearing after Pa and Tommy finished supper.

Matt drove all the way around the loop. For one horrible minute, Kathy thought he was going to leave, but to her relief, he started around again. In the center of the circle was a building with a sign: REST ROOMS. Across from it a big motor home was parked. Beside it was an empty campsite. Matt pulled in and turned off the engine.

"I gotta pee." He got out.

She was torn between getting out and her fear of the woods. The way he'd parked, all she could see was a thick wall of trees. Somewhere close, a child's laughter rang out, reassuring her. She reached for her hairbrush and little bag of cosmetics before she climbed out.

"Hi, there."

Kathy spun around. A woman standing on the road was smiling at her.

"I didn't mean to scare you, sorry." In the light from the rest rooms, she was young and pretty. She was wearing blue jeans and a plaid shirt, with a soft red sweater tied over her shoulders. Her light brown hair was pulled back in a ponytail.

"Hi," Kathy said.

The woman waved in the direction of the motor home. "We're in the next spot. I saw you drive in. Where're you from?"

"Oregon." It came out before Kathy had time to wonder if Matt would get mad at her for saying it.

"I'm Caroline Dodge. We're from Nebraska. Hubby Jim and two little monsters, Mike and Jamie." She waved vaguely toward the motor home again. "You don't by any chance have a couple of kids my boys can play with?" She laughed. "No such luck, huh? Well, I'm glad to have a new neighbor. We're staying three more days. How about you?"

Kathy glanced toward the rest rooms, but there was no sign of Matt. "I—I'm not sure."

"How about coming over for a beer? Jim can help your husband fill out the registration and give him some pointers. We've been here long enough to know the ropes."

Kathy smiled. Caroline's friendliness was a welcome change from Matt's moods. Maybe camping wouldn't be so bad if people were this nice. Shyly, she said, "My name's Kathy."

"Welcome to Bridge Bay, Kathy." Caroline smiled again and didn't ask for a last name.

Kathy wondered if Caroline had taken a good look at her, offering her a beer like that. She liked the idea of being taken for grown up. Caroline didn't look much older than Matt, but she had a husband and two kids. Kathy glanced toward the motor home and caught a glimpse of the man and two little boys through the trees. One of the boys looked about Tommy's age. When she turned back, Matt came out of the rest room. He stopped when he saw the woman, then crossed the road with quick strides, detouring around Caroline with his gaze fastened on Kathy.

Nervously she said, "This is our neighbor. She invited us over for a beer."

Matt hunched his shoulders, his back still to the road. Kathy saw the tic at the corner of his mouth. Caroline jammed her hands in her pockets.

"Listen, no sweat if you don't feel like it. We were exhausted the night we pulled in. We'll be there if you feel like coming over, okay?" She gave a jaunty wave and ambled back toward the motor home.

When she was out of earshot, Matt whirled on Kathy. "How come you talked to her?" he demanded, grabbing her arm.

"She just stopped—"

"Did she ask a lot of nosy questions?"

"No. Matt, you're hurting me." She tried to pull away, but his fingers were like claws.

"What'd you tell her?"

Kathy's anger began to ooze back. "Nothing. My name and that we're from Oregon."

"What else?" He pulled her so close she could feel his heart beating fast.

"Nothing. Honest, Matt. Ow—stop it!" She pried at his fingers. "For Pete's sake, what difference does it make? Anyone can see the license plates. She was just being nice." His grip loosened. She'd have black and blue marks on her arm. She rubbed the spot gingerly as her irritation spilled out of bounds. "Besides, I don't see why we have to live like gophers burying ourselves all the time. I'm sick of—"

He slammed her against the side of the van and pressed his arm across her throat, pinning her. "What are you sick of?"

She gasped for breath. In the faint glow of light across the road, Matt's eyes looked like thin ice with dark, freezing water under it.

"What are you sick of, Katie?" he demanded.

She swallowed. "Nothing. I didn't mean it. I was just talking."

For a moment, he didn't move. Finally the pressure on her windpipe eased. He could have killed her. What was the matter with him? She rubbed her throat and swallowed experimentally.

Matt's whisper was like a knife. "Watch out, Katie. Don't make me mad."

Her stomach flipflopped. "I won't, Matt. I promise." The wild look in his eyes scared her. How was she supposed to know what would make him mad next? Tomorrow, when it was light, she'd tell him she wanted to go home. If he wouldn't take her, she'd go anyhow. Hitchhike. It would be better than staying with someone who one minute told her he loved her and the next almost choked her. She'd go home no matter what. If Pa didn't let her in, she'd get by. She'd get a job. Wait table at the Sunset Cafe. Or get live-in work at one of the big houses on the summit where the rich mill owners lived. She could cook and clean . . . take care of kids. . . .

From the next campsite, the man's voice carried. "Okay, you two, quit running. Mikey, go get me a can of beer."

Matt walked around the van and peered through the trees that separated the campsites. He cocked his head as he watched the man fuss over a portable barbecue grill.

Kathy blew out her breath. What was the matter with him? He was as bad as Pa. Except her father made her work all the time. Maybe that was her trouble. She wasn't used to being idle. It took only a few minutes to straighten up the van every morning. No dishes to wash, no chores to do. She wondered how long it took Caroline to clean the motor home. She wondered what it was like inside. Just like a house, she bet. There were lights glowing in the windows. Did they have electricity? Maybe a generator or batteries.

Matt looked at her. "They invited us for a beer, huh?"

She nodded, still not trusting him.

"I could use a beer. Come on."

Amazed, she fell in step as he headed for the Dodge campsite. Caroline hailed them warmly.

"Hi, you two! Glad you could make it. Jim, these are our neighbors, Kathy and—Sorry, I didn't get your name."

"Pete," Matt said. "Pete Hanson."

"Well, hi, Pete. I'm Caroline and this is Jim." The man laid aside a long-handled barbecue fork and put out his hand.

"Hi. Hope you guys are going to hang around awhile.

We can use some young blood." He poked a thumb at the nearby darkened campsite and lowered his voice to a whisper. "Most folks around here go to bed with the chickens." He laughed as two little boys raced around the corner of the motor home almost colliding with Kathy. Jim grabbed them expertly, bringing them up short. "This is Jamie, and the curlyhead is Mike. Say hello, boys."

The two boys mumbled dutifully and scampered away as soon as he loosened his grip. They sprinted around the picnic table, knocking over one of the folding chairs at the edge of the clearing. Caroline righted it.

"Sit down," she said to Kathy. "I'll get some beer."

Kathy looked at the table. "If you're ready to eat—" The aroma of broiling chicken was rich in the air.

Caroline waved off the protest. "Plenty of time. We always feed the kids first so we can relax."

Jim said, "It'll be a half hour." He poked the fork into a piece of chicken, then picked up his beer and perched on a corner of the table. Kathy sat in one of the chairs but Matt stayed where he was. Kathy smiled at the little blond boy wriggling under the table to hide from his brother.

"Caroline says you're from Oregon," Jim said. "Eugene, by any chance? I have a buddy who lives up there."

"No," Matt said.

"Where are you from?" Jim persisted.

"Portland."

Kathy was relieved when Caroline returned. Why was Matt making up such a story? Neither of them had ever been to Portland. Suppose Jim or Caroline asked questions about it? Caroline passed around the beers, and Kathy busied herself with the pop top.

"I've never been to Portland," Jim said. "Never been in Oregon, for that matter. My buddy says it's God's country. One of these trips we'll get over that far." He drained the beer and dropped the can in a plastic sack under the table, then popped himself a fresh one. "What line are you in, Pete?"

"I run a feed store."

Liar. He was making up a whole new life for them, even giving himself a new name. Kathy felt as if she was watching a movie, not sure what was coming next. She sipped the frosty beer, wondering if it would make her drunk. She'd never had any kind of liquor except for the sips of homemade cherry wine her mother used to give her when she had a cold.

Mikey let out a whoop as he cornered Jamie under the table. With a practiced motion, Caroline grabbed both of them as they wriggled out. "Okay, you two, bedtime."

"Aw, Ma—"

"Get your pajamas on and brush your teeth, then you can listen to the radio for a little while. But no more noise, you hear? People are sleeping." She shooed them toward the door. When it closed behind them, she sank into the chair beside Kathy and raised her beer. "Happy hour," she declared with a laugh. "I adore them, but they run me ragged. Wait until you two have your own!"

Kathy drew a circle in the moisture on her beer can. Caroline raised her eyebrows. "Oh-oh, did I goof?" Kathy was aware of Caroline's quick glance at her unringed hand. "You two aren't married?" She looked at Matt.

Jim laughed. "You're smart, Pete." When Caroline made a playful jab at him, Jim ducked. "No kidding. Marry in haste, repent in leisure, I always say. Caroline and I lived together a year before we made it legal. Everybody does these days. It's better that way. It takes time to get to know each other and make sure you really want to spend the rest of your life together."

"Darn right," Caroline agreed.

The rest of her life . . . Kathy had never thought that far ahead. Did she want to spend the rest of her life with Matt, with his unpredictable bursts of rage and violence? She wondered if Jim ever hit Caroline. Somehow she had the feeling he didn't. She never realized before how people gave off a feeling of calmness or turbulence. Caroline and Jim were calm ones.

"How long you had the motor home?" Matt asked.

"Three years. When you've got kids, vacations are expensive if you stay in motels. We decided it would pay for itself in pretty short order. It saves us a bundle," Jim said.

"Is it hard to drive?"

"Nothing to it. Easy as a car once you get used to making wide corners. The mileage isn't great, but it's still a good investment for a family that wants to see the country before they get too old to enjoy it."

"Me and Katie are gonna get one," Matt said.

Kathy lifted the beer to hide her surprise. She wondered if Jim knew it was a lot of bull? Would they be riding and sleeping in a beat-up old van if they could afford a motor home?

"I have to check on the boys," Caroline said. "Come on, Kathy, I'll show you the inside."

Kathy shot Matt a questioning glance, but he wasn't looking at her. She got up and followed Caroline. Behind them, Matt and Jim started talking about prices and kinds of motor homes.

Kathy was astonished by the neat interior. She'd never seen anything so compact and cozy. There were two seats up front, like the van, but the rest of the space was just like a pretty little house on wheels. There were chairs, a couch, end tables, lamps, and a dining table that folded down out of the way. The whole kitchen with all the appliances fitted into a few feet of space. You could stand at the stove and reach anything you wanted. Caroline showed her the neat racks inside the cupboards that kept things in place. There was a tiny bathroom with a sink and toilet. Caroline explained how the shower worked. With Kathy still marveling, Caroline showed her the bedroom at the back. It was bigger than Kathy's room at home.

"Wow!" Kathy shook her head. "It's super!"

"The couch makes into a bed for the boys. I put them

down here, then Jim moves them when we're ready to turn in. This mountain air keeps them running on high all day, but they crash early.''

"I've never seen anything like it," Kathy said honestly. "No wonder you like to travel. Who wouldn't in something like this?" She ran her hand along a birch doorframe that was as smooth as the pews in church.

Caroline opened the refrigerator and took out four more beers. On the sofa, the two boys began scuffling. She set the beers on the counter. "Okay, you two, bedtime."

"Aw, Ma—"

"Bed. You're going fishing tomorrow with Dad, remember?"

"Oh boy!" They tumbled toward the bedroom, still scuffling playfully.

Caroline sighed. "I'll make sure they settle down. I'll only be a minute." She followed them into the bedroom.

Kathy touched the Formica counter top and the surface of the gleaming yellow refrigerator. Everything was so cheerful and pretty. She sat in one of the armchairs, swiveling slowly as she tried to imagine herself living here. The Dodges must be rich. A rig like this cost a fortune. She swung the chair around and looked at the fancy, expensive radio on the table. She'd seen pictures of those special portables once. It was the kind that picked up signals no matter where you were. There was hardly any static at all as she listened to the newscaster who had just come on. He was talking about a murder and robbery. Police were looking for a white van that had been parked at the Wee Rest Motel, where a bundle of bloody clothes had been found in the woods. Kathy sat up. The Wee Rest Motel. That was where—

The radio snapped off abruptly. Kathy jumped. She hadn't heard Matt come in. He was just there, looking at her with a funny expression. She licked her lips and tried to smile.

"Jim wants the salt," he said in a tight voice.

From the bedroom, Caroline yelled, ''It's right there on the counter next to the stove. Take the beers. I'll be right out.''

Matt picked up the salt and cans and waited for Kathy to go out ahead of him.

33

Kay was aware of the murmuring sound a long time before she opened her eyes. It was dark. She lay very still, confused by her aching body as she struggled up from deep, feverish sleep. There was something familiar about the sound her mind tried to reject. It was real, yet it was part of the nightmare she wanted to escape.

She ran her tongue over her cracked lips as she tried to focus her thoughts. Her flesh was burning. Had she been sick? Was she in a hospital? She studied the darkness, trying to identify the room. She was in a bed, but where? Not her own bed with Elliot beside her. But she had seen Elliot, hadn't she? The image blurred, and she moaned softly. Cautiously she reached out and felt a small warm figure. Jeff.

As memory flooded back, she remembered the terrifying darkness as Matt closed the trunk lid. Where had Jeff been? She ran her hand gently over his damp hair and warm face. He was all right—Matt hadn't hurt him. She sobbed softly. It was worse than a nightmare. Matt was driving her to madness. She felt it tightening around her, luring her with the promise of forgetfulness. So many things she didn't want to remember . . . so many. . . .

She listened again to the murmuring sound outside. In the nightmare, she'd been moving. Since she was no longer in the car trunk, that much was true. She turned to study a subtle change in the darkness. A window? Another one at the foot of the bed. Moonlight. Faint and eerie. Making grotesque patterns beyond the glass. Trees. Woods. She began to tremble. The soft, muted murmur. A waterfall.

34

Caroline tried to coax them to stay and finish their beers, but Matt insisted they had to go. Kathy muttered a quick apology as Matt herded her back to the van like a delinquent kid. He was mad, and she was frightened. Really frightened this time. She couldn't forget the look on Matt's face as he stood by the radio staring at her. The news broadcast played like a broken record inside her head: murder and robbery . . . white van . . . the Wee Rest Motel . . . She must have heard wrong. The sound had been low. Lots of motels had funny names.

Matt backed the van out. The wheels spun in the gravel as he hit the road. Kathy closed her eyes and tried not to be sick. She'd heard wrong, she must have. Coincidence. Not them. It couldn't be. Not Matt. Matt loved her. She hadn't been listening carefully, that was all. Caroline and the kids talking in the bedroom, Jim's rumbling voice outside. Sure, she'd heard wrong.

Matt was hunched over the wheel, his shoulders almost touching his hands, staring ahead as if he was carving the road out of the darkness. There was a steady tic in the muscle of his jaw. The pale moonlight painted his flesh a ghostly green-white. Kathy shuddered and pressed her hand over her mouth.

Matt twisted the wheel sharply, almost sending her

175

flying. She grabbed the door as they bumped onto a rough road. Suddenly the moonlight was gone. She couldn't see the lake anymore, only woods and the terrifying darkness. "Where are we going?" She grabbed his arm.

He knocked her hand away. "Shut up!"

"Let's go back to the campground. I don't care about the hotel—honest. Matt, don't take me into the woods! Matt, please—"

He backhanded her a stinging blow. "Shut up! Goddam it, I said shut up!"

"I won't! I'm scared. I hate the woods. I hate them! I want to go home!" The van lurched so suddenly, she fell against the door. Pain stung her shoulder and she began to cry.

Matt's breath hissed. "You can't go home. I told you, your pa don't want you."

"I don't care. I'll beg. I'll promise anything. He'll change his mind, you'll see." She hated Matt and the van and the woods. She wouldn't stay. She couldn't.

The van pitched and rocked but Matt didn't slow. He was driving like a stunt man in a chase movie. Kathy clung to the seat so she wouldn't be thrown against the dash. He was crazy. She wouldn't stay with him. The woods gathered the van into its dark arms. Kathy squeezed her eyes shut and tried to pray, but she couldn't remember the words to the simple prayer she'd said all her life. The prayer Mama had taught her. *Now I—*

The van stopped with a sickening lurch. Her eyes flew open. Matt was leaning on the wheel panting like a dog after a rabbit.

"Where are we?" It came out like a whisper in church. She glanced out the window, then looked away quickly. Matt didn't answer. "Matt, let's go back, please?"

"Can't. Your pa—"

"Not to Blue Canyon. To the campground. It was nice there. I liked Caroline and Jim. You did too. You were talking to him about the motor home and all."

He looked at her with narrowed eyes. "You like that stupid motor home better than the van, don't you?"

"Sure. I mean, no. It's different. It was nice—"

"You like them better'n you like me?" he demanded.

"No, of course not. They're just—people. A family. I don't even know them. How can I like them better than you?" The words tumbled out in panic. "We don't even have to talk to them if you don't want to. We'll just go back and park and sleep, okay?" The night crept closer and was tapping at the windows. Outside she could hear the faint sound of something moving.

Matt sneered. "Sure, so you can sneak out and go over there. I'm wise to you, Katie. You ain't gonna pull that on me again."

"I won't do anything like that, I swear! I can't stay here in the dark. I'm scared of the woods. I don't want to stay here—" She was crying, and she was going to be sick. She groped for the door handle, gagging on the terrible sourness in her throat. She got the door open and leaned out, retching. Matt grabbed her hair and jerked her back, pressing her neck against the seat back so she was looking up at the roof. Vomit surged into her mouth. A strangled sound came from her lips.

"You like them better than me 'cuz they got that motor home, don'cha!" His eyes glowed like coals at the back of a winter stove. Kathy tried to shake her head but she couldn't move. The pain in her tingling scalp drove away the nausea. Matt leaned close. "I done a lot for you, Katie. I ain't gonna let you go. You're mine, and don't you forget it." He moved, then his lips were on hers, wet and cruel and searching. She could taste her own vomit. When he let her go, she gasped for breath and shuddered.

"You cold?"

She nodded.

"Get in your sleeping bag."

She shook her head. "No. I don't want to—not here!" She felt him stiffen but his voice was calm.

"Go on, get in. It's warmer." He started to open the door.

"Where are you going?"

"I'll be right back. I gotta pee. Then we'll go, okay? Back to the campgrounds."

She gave a nervous gulp. "Really?"

He stood a moment at the open door. The night air surged in like rolling fog. "Sure, Katie. Now get in the sleeping bag before you catch cold. Go on."

She scrambled over the seat, willing to make peace as long as they didn't stay here. Matt shut the door. The click of the latch was loud in the sudden darkness as the overhead light went off. She unzipped the sleeping bag, shivering violently. The van had cooled quickly with the door open. Still she hesitated, the flap of the sleeping bag in one hand as she listened.

"Matt?"

She didn't hear him at all.

"Matt?" Her voice rang hollowly. "Matt, where are you?"

Outside, an echo whispered.

She climbed over the seat and peered out. Fumbling, she rolled the window down an inch and put her mouth close. "Matt!" She was screaming now. "Matt! Answer me! Don't leave me here alone! *Matt!*"

Something rustled in the brush. Clutching the window, Kathy stared into the darkness. "Matt?" It was a hoarse whisper. The sound came again, heavy and ominous. The shadows moved, dark on dark, terrifying. She rolled up the window and pushed the lock, then reached across to lock the driver's side. Matt was gone. He'd left her here alone. He was punishing her, getting even. He never meant it. He lied. He lied. The thing outside crashed in the brush, then was silent. There was only the quiet steady sound she couldn't identify. Terrified, she crept back and crawled into the sleeping bag. Squeezing her eyes shut, she pulled the flap over her head.

* * *

He took the flashlight out of the athletic bag but didn't turn it on. Once his eyes got used to the dark, he could see the road. Besides, he didn't want Katie to catch on. Let her sit there wondering. Served her right. He didn't like to punish her, but she had to learn. Yessir, she had to learn.

He walked softly, like a mountain cat stalking its prey. The darkness was cool against his face but he was plenty warm in the windbreaker. He was never cold in the dark. He was part of the night. It welcomed him and fed him. It was part of him.

There were still some lights in the campground. He avoided the road. Instead, he worked his way through the outer ring of woods, stepping lightly and pausing now and then to listen like an animal. Close to the motor home, he crouched in a thicket of young pines.

A few glowing coals were left in the grill, but the garbage sack was gone and the table cleared. A light was on in the living room where Katie had been listening to the radio. Were they listening to the radio? He cocked his head, but he didn't hear anything but the sounds of the night. Across the road, the light from the rest rooms glared in his eyes. It made it hard to see when he looked away. If he had an air rifle, he could shoot it out. He raised his arms and took imaginary aim. Bam! He had an air rifle once but Pa took it away.

The door of the motor home opened and Caroline and Jim came out carrying drinks. Jim pulled the two lawn chairs close together at the edge of the clearing where they were out of the light splashing across the road. When they sat down and Jim put his arm around her, Caroline laid her head on his shoulder. Jim said something that made her laugh. The tinkling sound drifted through the darkness.

When they finished the drinks, Jim rose and carried the glasses inside. Matt moved quickly and silently. He was behind Caroline before she turned. Her mouth rounded in surprise, then gave way to a smile as she recognized him.

"You're back—"

Matt jerked her by the hair and slashed the knife across her throat. The rest of her words burbled as blood spurted. When he let go, her head fell forward and came to rest as if she were staring at the dark stain spreading down her shirt. Matt wiped the knife on her jeans. Glancing at the motor home, he saw Jim's shadow at the door. Quickly, he stepped in front of Caroline and ducked the knife behind his back.

Jim looked startled. "Hey, I didn't hear you guys come back." He glanced toward the site where the van had been earlier. Giving Matt a puzzled look, he tried to see past him. "Caro—"

One step. The knife was part of Matt's arm. It sank deep in the soft flesh. Jim's mouth opened, and he shook his head as though Matt had asked a question. Matt pulled the knife out and shoved it in again. And again. And again. Jim buckled and fell, away from the knife, away from Matt. He thrashed weakly. Matt bent over him and stabbed his chest. He heard the knife scrape bone. Jim Dodge lay still.

Matt wiped the knife blade again and stuck it in his belt. Using both arms, he dragged Jim's body into the shadows behind Caroline's chair. The light washed across her hair, making it almost as golden as Katie's, and Matt smiled. Carefully, he took the red sweater from her shoulders and pushed it into the athletic bag. Then, pressing his hand against the knife under his windbreaker, he walked to the motor home.

35

Elliot jumped off the road as headlights came around a curve and pinned him in their glare. He felt the suck of air as a motor home passed. It wasn't going fast, but the driver veered dangerously, probably dozing at the wheel. *My own fault,* Elliot thought. In dark clothes, he was practically invisible. No driver would expect someone walking on the road in the middle of the night.

He reached the marina physically and emotionally drained. Harriet was right, there was nothing he could do until morning. If then. Frustration tormented him, but the long walk had exhausted him. He let himself in quietly. Taking off his jacket and shoes, he climbed into bed fully dressed and sank into haunted sleep.

He woke with the first streaks of dawn a few hours later. The motor home was cold. His breath made small puffs of moisture as he pulled on a heavy sweater. By the time he came out of the bathroom, Harriet was up. Her face was puffy but she gave him a cheerful smile.

"Did you get some sleep?"

"Enough."

"You don't look it. I'll put on some coffee." She filled the pot and measured coffee from a tin. Setting it on a burner, she adjusted the flame, then carried her clothes into the bathroom. When she emerged, she made breakfast, ignoring his protest that he wasn't hungry.

"That moonlight walk should have worked up an appetite."

He gave her a sheepish grin. "I thought I was being so quiet."

She smiled. "Where'd you go?"

He told her about the waterfall and Natural Bridge. Her brows rose speculatively. "And?"

"Zilch. I stumbled around in the dark for nothing. There was no sign of a car or anything else."

Harriet spread jam on a piece of toast. "Let's check with the ranger station. Bass may have some news."

The ranger station at Lake was buzzing with activity. Half a dozen park service trucks were pulled up close to the entrance and uniformed rangers congregated on the porch and inside. Elliot parked at the end of the line so he wouldn't block traffic.

A ranger saw them coming and held the door open. The tall, gray-haired man at the desk picked up the phone as it shrilled. His gaze found Elliot and Harriet, and he indicated chairs. The nameplate on the desk read JOHN MCGUIRE, DISTRICT RANGER.

He spoke into the phone. "They just came in." McGuire listened again, then said, "Right." He hung up. "Mr. Pier?" When Elliot nodded, McGuire said, "I was just going to send someone for you."

"What's happened?" Elliot demanded.

McGuire ignored the question. "I've got orders from Superintendent Bass to hold you here."

"What the hell for?"

"Superintendent Bass will explain. He's on his way."

"Damn it, you can't—"

"Sit down, Mr. Pier . . . ma'am. . . ." McGuire indicated chairs.

Elliot turned toward the door. "You can't hold us without cause."

"Mr. Pier—" McGuire drew a deep breath. "Sit down,

please. You're right. We have no legal authority to detain you, but I'd appreciate it if you'd stay and wait for the superintendent.''

''Not unless you tell me what this is all about,'' Elliot countered. Something had happened, something serious enough to bring Bass down here personally. Elliot fought the horrible certainty that it concerned Kay and Jeff.

McGuire was thoughtful a moment, then said, ''A man and wife were stabbed to death last night up at Canyon.''

Elliot sank into one of the wooden armchairs, his gaze frozen on the ranger.

''Their motor home was stolen. Presumably that was the motive.''

Elliot was having trouble with his stomach. Canyon. . . . He'd guessed wrong. He watched McGuire's florid face as he went on.

''The couple had dinner at the Center and came out of the restaurant about midnight. A half hour later, a guy felt a thump as he backed out his pickup.'' McGuire looked grim. ''The two bodies had been rolled under it.''

Elliot's tongue swelled like a sponge. He pushed out the word. ''Stabbed?''

McGuire nodded. ''I'm going to level with you, Mr. Pier,'' he said. ''There isn't much doubt it was Briggs.'' He picked up a pad on which he'd made notes. ''An FBI agent named Farmington has been in touch with Superintendent Bass. There have been two other killings out on County Road A2 and Route 20. A credit card with your wife's name on it was found near the gas pumps in a service station where the owner was slashed to death.''

Elliot heard Harriet's gasp and covered his eyes as pain seared his skull. Briggs was on another bloody rampage. He realized McGuire was talking again.

''A ranger found your wife's purse in a car parked on a service road up on North Rim Drive at Canyon this morning.''

The last doubt was erased. Briggs was in the park, and

he had Kay and Jeff. And now a motor home. A warning bell sounded deep in Elliot's mind, rousing memories. The Dodges had a motor home. Briggs and Kathy had seen it, been in it—Kathy had admired the Dodges' rig, and Briggs had been furious. He'd gone back and killed an entire family in a rage. Another piece of the hazy puzzle suddenly cleared and fell in place. Matt was going to steal the motor home, but he couldn't find the keys. When a light went on in the next trailer, he panicked and ran, taking only the radio and Caroline Dodge's bloodstained sweater. It had been the beginning of their hard running. Every cop in six states had their description then. Briggs stole cars and food along a four-state path, and they holed up in remote areas where they lived like animals. Until Barstow, where Briggs pushed his luck once too often. The rest was history.

McGuire said, "We're bringing in every man we can round up, and the gates are covered. We've got a hundred people looking for that Winnebago with North Dakota plates."

Elliot heard a buzzing sound inside his head. McGuire looked at him peculiarly.

"Are you okay, Mr. Pier?"

Elliot rubbed his temple. "What time did you say those people were killed?"

"Midnight or a little after."

He and Harriet had gotten to Bridge Bay about midnight. They'd turned in almost immediately, and it hadn't been long afterward that he went out. One? One-thirty?

"Jesus—"

Harriet's face was pale as he looked at her.

"Coming back last night, a motor home passed me just as I turned in. It was going slow. It hit the shoulder, and I thought the driver was dozing at the wheel. *But he had the wrong spot!* He mistook the marina road for the one to Natural Bridge!"

Harriet whispered, "Briggs?"

Elliot bolted for the door.

"Pier—hold it!" McGuire commanded.

"He's got my wife and son—"

McGuire said firmly, "We've got men on the way who know these woods and roads. Leave it to us."

Elliot shook his head. "I hear you, and I need all the help you can give, but don't try to stop me."

McGuire said, "I've got orders." A burly ranger blocked the door.

Harriet took Elliot's arm. "Listen to him, Elliot. We've got to put Kay and Jeff's safety above everything."

"They'll go in like gangbusters, damn it. I have to get Kay and Jeff out before Briggs knows he's trapped. He'll go berserk."

She turned to McGuire. "Send someone with him."

McGuire gnawed the idea, then motioned to the man blocking the door. "Go with him, Sam, but no heroics, you hear?" Sam Feeney nodded and followed Elliot out.

36

It was still dark when Kay opened her eyes again. Foggily, she tried to decide if it was the same night. It seemed too long, but she couldn't have slept through an entire day. She examined the gray half-light and decided it was almost dawn. Morning. She had to get up and—What? What did she have to do?

She moved like an awkward puppet controlled by a novice hand. She felt the thin sheen of sweat on her face. Fever . . . Had she been sick long? She studied the hazy gray room but it told her nothing.

She felt a movement beside her and looked at the humped covers. A spike of golden hair poked from under the edge of the quilt. She pulled back the blanket and touched Jeff's face. His skin was hot and dry. His breathing was a shallow pant.

Fragments of memory began to stir. Matt locking her in the car trunk—She looked around. Windows . . . a door . . . Not a house . . . A motor home! Matt had locked her in the car trunk while he went for a motor home.

She was sucked into a spiral of terror. *He couldn't find the keys—Someone had come along—Dead, all four of them—Oh, God, no, no, no!*

That was the past, eleven years ago. But Matt was living in the past, trying to drag her back with him into his fantasy world where . . .

Through the predawn quiet, she heard the soft sound of

the waterfall. The same spot. He'd returned like a migrating bird to its nesting place. As though the years hadn't intervened, she heard Matt's plaintive sobbing. *"I wanted it for you, Katie. A comfortable bed and no more washing up in cold streams, you said. But I couldn't find the keys. Why would he hide the keys, for crisake? I looked all over, even in the bedroom with those two brats lying there."*

"You left me alone for spite! I hate you, Matt Briggs, I hate you! I want to go home!"

"You can't go home. I told you—"

"I don't care what Pa said. He'll take me back, you'll see."

"He won't!"

"He will!"

"He won't. He can't. He's dead!"

Kay forced herself to breathe through her mouth until the nausea passed, then sat up slowly. The bedsprings creaked. Jeff gave a whimpering sigh.

Where was Matt? Cautiously she put her feet over the side of the bed. She was still wearing her shoes and clothes. After the warm bed, the red sweater was worthless against the chill.

"I brought you a present, Katie. Red's your favorite color."

"That's Caroline's!"

"She doesn't need it anymore. Put it on, Katie. It'll keep you warm."

She stood up slowly. Her legs tingled with the sudden rush of blood, and she put a hand on the wall to steady herself. The bedroom door was ajar. She listened, but there was nothing but Jeff's scratchy breathing and the distant sound of the waterfall. She opened the door. She could barely make out the indistinct outlines of furniture. Beyond the windows, the day hadn't gathered enough light to dispel the shadows. Still lightheaded, she took a cautious step, feeling her way past the bath and kitchen until she could see the living room. There was a dark hump on the couch.

Matt. Sleeping with his face turned to the wall, a blanket pulled over his head like a child burrowing in fear.

Was he asleep or pretending, waiting for her to move before he leaped up and grabbed her? Her heart thundered as she took a cautious step. Matt didn't move. Her gaze slid around the gloom. The door was directly across from him. Was it locked? She took a step but stopped as Matt drew a deep, sighing breath. She froze until she was sure he hadn't wakened. She'd only have one chance. There was no time to inspect the lock. She'd have to risk it with Jeff in her arms. She backed into the bedroom.

Jeff's eyelids were waxy and his mouth open as he breathed with tiny gasps. She had to keep him warm, but the quilt was too heavy and awkward to manage. She groped in the curtained storage space above the bed and found a heavy wool jacket. Pulling back the blankets, she rolled Jeff into it. When he stirred, she put a hand over his mouth. He settled listlessly into the warm nest.

Staggering under his weight, she made her way back to the living room. Five feet to the door. Don't think about it. One step at a time. Jeff's weight numbed her arms. The whisper of the woolen jacket against her clothes sounded loud, but Matt didn't stir. One more step . . . step down for the door. Cold. Don't think about it. The lock? Her fingers moved along the frame, searching for the door handle. The latch clicked. She pushed the door open and stepped out. Cold air hit her like a blow. She stumbled along the length of the motor home as leaves and twigs snapped under her feet like a string of firecrackers. She should have closed the door—Then suddenly she was out in the open. She ran.

"Katie!" The muffled shout exploded in the quiet.

Terror-stricken, she veered from the road and plunged into the woods. Branches whipped and snagged at her. The faint predawn didn't penetrate the dense forest, and she blundered blindly. She couldn't stop, not for a moment. Gasping for breath, she tried to shift Jeff's weight, but her foot tangled in a root and she fell against a tree. Jeff began to whimper. She hugged him, muffling the sound. How far had she come? Not far enough. Matt could run faster—She plunged on, no longer sure which direction she was going. She tried to listen for sounds of pursuit, but her own thrashing was so loud she couldn't hear anything else. *It doesn't matter—keep going. . . don't stop . . . get away . . . only one chance. . . .*

She leaned against a tree to catch her breath as the cold air raked her lungs. She couldn't feel her arms locked around Jeff anymore, only the heat of his fevered body.

A noise—She peered into the cloying forest, listening, trying to detect the slightest movement. Was it Matt? Could he see her? Was he out there, waiting? She began to shiver with a terror worse than the cold. Without warning, Matt's voice shattered the quiet.

"Don't make me mad, Katie. I'm gonna find you, you know I will."

She held her breath. His voice carried clearly, but it came from a distance. Which direction? Was he near enough to hear her moving?

"Katie? You promised it would be okay when we got to Yellowstone. You wanted a motor home, remember? Everything is going to be perfect, you promised."

Walk . . . he'll find you if you stay here . . . he can see in the dark . . . move . . . now. . . .

"I wanted it for you, Katie. You said it was just like a real home. If that stupid Jim hadn't hid the keys. Damn it. Why'd he do that? Don't cry, Katie, you're gonna make me mad! It wasn't my fault! I'll get one, you'll see. It'll be better. . . . Everything will be perfect, you promised!"

A light. The sun coming up. Over the lake. East. The road. Run!

She stumbled and fell heavily. Jeff began to cry. *Get up. Keep going.* The light—It slithered and leaped among the trees as she struggled to her knees. The pain in her leg was unbearable. The light was coming closer. Not the sun. A flashlight! *Oh, God*—She scrambled to her feet, ignoring the pain. She ran. The branch of a huge pine caught her across the forehead. The ground pitched and she staggered helplessly, then fell to the cold, damp ground.

37

Feeney pulled over and shut off the ignition. The early morning hush closed over the fading sound of the engine.

"We're a half mile from the falls." He looked down the road speculatively.

"Is there any other way out?" Elliot's gaze searched the road he'd walked last night.

"There's a service trail that runs a couple of miles but you need a four-wheel drive. If he's got a motor home, he's got to come out this way."

Dawn was imminent, and a gray misty light filtered through the trees. Kay and Jeff had been with Briggs forty-eight hours. A lifetime, and Briggs had a knife. They'd have to take him by surprise before he could use it.

"I'm going down there," Elliot said, opening the door.

Feeney grabbed his arm. "Our men will be here in twenty minutes."

Elliot shook off the ranger's hand and slid out of the cab. Feeney leaned across the seat, whispering fiercely. "Our men will be armed. It's crazy to confront a kill-er—"

Elliot started down the road. It was easier going than it had been last night. He walked softly, alert to every flutter in the wakening forest. He saw the loop when he was a good hundred yards from it. He stopped to study both forks, then approached slowly. No wonder he'd blundered last night. The road branched abruptly, with one path climbing steeply to the left. The other followed a level route around a thicket. The waterfall was in the niche of a cutback, almost invisible. He caught only an occasional flash of white froth as it splashed down the rocks. He listened to the faint sound. Above him, a bird burst into sudden welcome of the day. There was nothing else. No voices, no sound of movement. He inched ahead until he could see past the brush. In the gray gloom of the clearing, a motor home was parked in a small turnout.

Numb, he studied the square, clean lines of the Winnebago. It was the same one that had passed him last night, he was sure. It took all his control not to bolt across the clearing. The curtains were drawn, and he couldn't see the door. There was no sign of life. He studied the clearing. Crossing it, he'd be out in the open for thirty feet. It was too risky. On the high side of the loop, the woods that ran close to the narrow road were still in deep shadows. If he got around far enough, he'd be able to see the door and windshield. He made his way up, pausing now and then to listen, unable to shake off his gnawing fear. Then he was at a high point, looking down at the motor home.

Panic hit him with the impact of a blow. The door of the Winnebago was wide open. No longer worried about noise, he plunged down the hillside. He grabbed the doorframe and swung himself inside, his body tense. A blanket at the end of the couch lay half on the floor. The room was empty. He dashed to the bedroom. The blankets were rumpled as if someone had thrown them back hastily. Elliot yanked them off, then dropped them in a heap as he turned away. They'd been here. But where were they now? He went outside and stood listening to the forest. There was an expectancy—a high-power tension in the ominous quiet.

He scanned the woods, the clearing, the cutback where the waterfall danced down the rocks.

Suddenly a sound sliced through the morning stillness. Elliot went rigid. A shout—Feeney? It had been muffled and indistinct. On a dead run, Elliot took off down the road.

38

Kay tried to swim out of the sea of pain. It seeped through her body and leadened her limbs. She longed to sink back into the warm comfort of darkness, but she sensed the danger. She struggled to open her eyes. She was lying on the ground clutching a bundle. Jeff—She peeled back the coat to make sure he was all right.

She'd been running—fallen . . . How long had she been lying here? Where was Matt? She glanced around and listened to the whispering woods. Was that a step? She pressed her hand to her mouth. She had to keep moving. Where was Matt when he yelled? She searched for the bobbing beam of the flashlight, but the woods had gotten light enough that he didn't need it now. She sat up cautiously, expecting Matt to materialize in the shadows. Which way had she been going? *Think, Kay, think!* The sun would be up soon and she and Jeff would be a clear target.

The sun! It rose on the other side of the lake! There was a road around the lake! That direction—head for the brightest sky.

She got to her knees and tried to lift Jeff. He was so quiet. Let him sleep. *If I should die before I wake . . .*

The pine boles blurred and wavered. She had to get Jeff to a doctor. Jeff needed a doctor. *Mama needed a doctor . . . run . . .* She groaned silently and leaned against a tree until the pain in her leg subsided. Finally she stood, doubled with Jeff's weight. Toward the sun. *Hurry. There's not much time.* Wobbling like a newborn calf, she hit a tree and almost fell again. Sobbing, she propelled herself from one tree to the next, managing to stay on her feet. Pain became part of her so she could no longer isolate it.

Matt stepped in her path so suddenly, she bumped into him before she saw him. He was smiling, and his eyes burned like coals in the deep sockets under his brows. Behind him the woods turned red with a sudden glow. Blood red.

Kay's mouth opened in a soundless scream.

39

"Mama, I brought you a cup of tea." Kathy set the tray by the bed. Her mother smiled but didn't open her eyes. Kathy kissed the cool, dry cheek. "I fixed it the way you showed me, Mama. I warmed the pot and used boiling water."

Her mother's eyelids fluttered and her thin lips moved. "You're a good girl, Kathy."

"Can you sit up and drink it?" Kathy slid an arm under her mother's shoulders and tried to raise her on the pillows. Mama's breath caught.

"I have to get up," she said unsteadily.

"The doctor said—" The doctor said complete bed rest. Mama was worn out after the baby. She wasn't supposed to do anything. But as soon as the doctor left, Pa wanted his supper. Ranch women had babies and went back to work the same day, he told her. None of that mollycoddling for a week in the hospital and hiring help when you got home. Mama didn't argue. Kathy didn't either, though she hated Pa for it. Anyone could see Mama was sick. It had been a hard pregnancy and a difficult delivery, even though the baby was perfect in every way. It wasn't his fault, poor tyke. Kathy changed him and rocked him when he fretted so Mama could rest, and she brought him to be nursed when he howled with hunger. When she was home from school, she did as many of Mama's chores as she could, but somehow it was never enough to satisfy Pa.

"Help me, Kathy. Bring my robe like a good girl."
Mama threw back the covers and put her feet over the side
of the bed. Kathy knelt and put the slippers on Mama's
cold feet, then helped her into her robe. With an arm
around her waist, she got Mama up. Mama swayed but
Kathy held tight. She was strong for a girl of ten. Mama
depended on her. As they started across the room slowly,
Mama moaned suddenly.

"Are you all right, Mama?" Kathy saw that Mama's
face was white as snow. Her lids were waxy as she closed
her eyes, and her mouth was a thin, faint scar. *"Mama!"*

Mama's full weight dragged on Kathy's arm as she began to fall. Sobbing, Kathy pulled her toward the bed.
*"You shouldn't have gotten up. I shouldn't have let you.
Mama . . . Mama . . ."* Kathy let her down on the bed.
Bending to lift Mama's legs, Kathy saw the blood. A big
pool where Mama had stopped . . . a red trail all the way
back to the bed.

"Mama!"

Her mother's eyes didn't open as her lips moved. *"Help
me, Kathy . . ."* she gasped as she clutched her middle.
"Get Pa—hurry—"

Kathy ran. Past the blood. Out of the house. Across the
yard. She threw herself over the fence, not caring when
she heard her blouse rip. Not caring about anything but
getting help for Mama. She started across the freshly
plowed field, stumbling in the furrows, falling flat and getting to her feet and plunging on blindly. She had to get
help.

Panting, she stopped and raised her hand to her eyes as
she searched the field. When she finally saw the tractor, it
was a tiny speck against the sun. She started to run into
the blood-red sunset.

40

Feeney was running toward him, gun drawn. Panting, Feeney pointed. "It came from that direction!" He grabbed Elliot when he would have plunged into the woods.

"Captain McGuire and Superintendent Bass are on the way. I just talked to them on the CB." He lifted his ear to the morning breeze. "That's them. Come on, we'll meet them at the truck."

Elliot hesitated, peering toward the forest that was still in deep shadows. Feeney hadn't shouted. Briggs? Why? At whom? When Feeney tugged his arm, Elliot went along reluctantly.

Bass and McGuire were climbing out of a park truck with half a dozen rangers in back. Elliot told them about the Winnebago. The superintendent turned to one of his men. "Check the license and keep an eye on it. Stay out of sight. He may double back."

The ranger set off down the road at a brisk pace. Bass gave McGuire curt orders. "Throw a net around the area. Stop traffic on the highway and make sure no one comes in this road. Post men at the campgrounds and marina in case he heads that way." Bass turned back to Elliot and Feeney. "Where did the shout come from?"

Feeney said, "The south side of the road. It was in front of me, I'd guess a quarter of a mile."

Elliot realized how much more discerning Feeney had been. A man who knew the woods.

Bass deployed the rest of his men, who fanned out and entered the woods at intervals.

"You stay put, Pier."

"No way."

Bass gave him a hard look. "Okay, then stick with me. I don't need you getting lost. Understood?"

Elliot agreed with newfound respect for the park system and the men who ran it. And the holstered gun on Bass's hip added a sense of security. It would help even the sides.

41

The smell of damp rotting earth choked her. Pa had hit her for running in front of the tractor. She had to get up, had to tell him about Mama. *Get help . . . hurry . . .*

The thought swam away in an ocean of red. She was no longer in that distant place. She moved, trying to grasp reality. *Get help . . . hurry . . .*

"Why'd you run away, Katie?"

Her eyes flew open. Matt was hunkered down beside her, the butcher knife in his hand. Beside him, Jeff was propped against a rotting log. The mackinaw had fallen open, and he was pale and limp. Matt flicked the knife against Jeff's shoe.

"Don't scream, Katie. I mean it."

She clamped her teeth.

"I don't understand you," Matt said in a puzzled tone. His face was strangely calm, except for his eyes, which seemed to burn into her. "I got you the motor home like I promised. Why'd you run out? You can't go now, you know that, don't you?" When she didn't respond, he punched her shoulder. "Answer me!"

She nodded helplessly, forcing herself not to look at Jeff. There was no one to help. It was up to her.

"Remember how it was, Katie? Just you and me. Nothing else mattered, remember?"

She bit her lip until the uncontrollable shiver passed.

Scowling, Matt glanced at Jeff. "You said you missed

Tommy, so I let him come this time. Now you're trying to run away again. I don't understand you, Katie.'' He moved the knife along Jeff's leg, catching the hem of the cotton pants and slitting the cloth with a quick motion. Kay gasped.

Matt leaned toward her. ''Remember that day by the stream when we made love the first time? I wanted you so bad, Katie. I was happier right then than I'd ever been in my whole life.''

He had slipped completely into his fantasy world. The polished bits of memory had become what he wanted them to be. He believed they'd been lovers. He believed she'd waited for him, that she wanted him now.

''You liked the sound of the water, remember?'' He grinned. ''You liked so many things. I'm going to get them all for you, Katie, just see if I don't.''

The red sweater . . . the radio . . . the motor home . . .

He looked at her as though the past ten years had never been. ''I knew you'd wait, just like you promised.''

She licked her cracked lips and forced the words from her tongue. ''That was so long ago.'' They came out in a soft whisper he mistook for intimacy.

He put his hand under her shoulders, lifting her and drawing her into his arms. ''I couldn't get back any sooner, Katie. I wanted to, but they wouldn't let me. Juhnny said I had to do it their way, but they lied to me. They promised, but they lied!'' He let her go suddenly and stabbed the knife into the ground. ''Liars! They don't want us to be together.'' He plunged the knife into the hard dirt again, then pulled it out and wiped it carefully on his jeans.

She chose words carefully. ''But you came back.'' When he looked at her, she forced a smile. ''You didn't let them stop you, no matter what they said.''

''Yeah.'' He looked as if she'd confirmed something important.

Nervously, Kay folded her arms across her breasts. ''It's

cold. Let's go back.'' She prayed desperately that he didn't see how scared she was.

Matt looked confused, then pleased. "I remembered about the motor home. You like it, don't you?"

"It's very nice. The nicest I've ever seen," she said quickly so he wouldn't make comparisons. "Why don't we go back there? I'll make some coffee.''

When he turned to look at Jeff, Kay's breath caught. She said quickly, "Just the two of us, Matt. We don't want anyone else." The words choked her. Matt slapped the knife against his palm. Kay scrambled to her feet. "Leave Tommy here. He doesn't matter anymore."

When Matt hesitated, Kay linked her arm through his. He took a step, then pulled back, shaking his head. Kay forced herself to say the words he wanted to hear.

"It'll be better now, Matt, you'll see."

"It'll be better, you'll see. We'll have a comfortable bed and a shower and everything you want, Katie. A motor home's better than a house 'cause you can take it wherever you want to go. We'll be free, Katie. You and me. Just you and me. Lovers forever. . . ."

She coaxed him a step, then another. He looked at her with a dazed expression, as if he couldn't believe the long struggle was over. Kay led him away from Jeff.

42

The virgin forest was a wild place, with sparse, twisted undergrowth where the sun didn't penetrate. Fallen logs and decaying leaves constantly regenerated life. In the chilly morning mist, it had a rank smell. Elliot listened for the other searchers, but the thick carpet of pine needles covering the forest floor deadened sound. They were men trained in the woods, he thought. Observant. His own gaze flitted randomly, unable to pierce the shadows. He could be within reach of Kay and Jeff and not see them. If Briggs had hurt them, he'd kill him. The hell with a system of justice that should have taken that useless life. He'd make sure Briggs never—

Bass touched his shoulder and put a finger to his lips. Elliot strained to hear what had alerted him, but there was only the faint whisper of the wind. He looked at Bass questioningly. The chief ranger motioned him to follow. Bass moved quietly for a big man. Elliot tried to imitate his soft tread. When Bass shot out his arm in warning, Elliot halted. The superintendent pointed to a thin branch of a young pine that lay broken against the ground. He squatted, studying the twisted boughs and running his hand lightly over the scuffed pine needles.

Bass set out again, moving like a scout before a wagon train. Elliot couldn't harness his fears for Kay and Jeff anymore. They were out here somewhere. He had to find the two people he loved most in the world before a crazed killer—

Bass stopped again and drew Elliot down as he sank to his haunches. Without disturbing the brush, he pointed to a spot a few yards ahead. Elliot squinted. A fallen log. He made it out then: the outline of a head. Someone was sitting against the log. Bass drew his gun and signaled their move, Elliot to the left, himself to the right. They rose and moved slowly.

One figure. Which of them? One figure, and it hadn't moved. Sweat trickled under the collar of Elliot's jacket. He judged his distance and paused. Where the hell was that log? He proofread the shadows until he found the dark line he was looking for. And the figure. Across from him, Bass broke through the undergrowth, gun aimed as Elliot caught a glimpse of Jeff's pale face. He dived through the brush, his heart pounding.

"Don't shoot—it's my son!" He knelt and lifted Jeff's limp form. Elliot pressed his face against the small pale one. "Christ, he's burning with fever." He pulled the heavy woolen coat around Jeff. Glancing around, he gave Bass an agonized look. "Where's Kay?"

"Let's get the boy back to the truck," Bass said.

Kay couldn't be far if she'd left Jeff here. Dazed, Elliot got to his feet and stumbled after the ranger.

Bass brought them out of the woods a few yards from the trucks. Two more had joined the lineup. Harriet rushed toward them.

She checked Jeff with a worried expression. "Where's Kay?"

Elliot's voice choked. "She wasn't with him."

"Give him to me. We'll radio for a doctor."

Elliot kissed Jeff's hot cheek and passed over the precious burden. Harriet hurried to one of the trucks where a ranger sat with a radio mike in his hand. Elliot saw Bass talking to Herb Farmington. So he finally came. *Supercop,* Elliot thought angrily. If Farmington had listened to him, they might have prevented this. Now the FBI would be as much help as an outbreak of bubonic plague.

Bass turned as a radio cackled, listened, then motioned to Elliot. "That was my man watching the motor home. Your wife and Briggs just came back. They're inside now."

43

Matt moved through the woods with an instinct born of the loner. Kay was numb. The protective dam had split, releasing the murky waters of the past, but Jeff was safe. Someone would find him and help him more than she could. He was safe from Matt.

Matt led her down the slope to the motor home, grabbing her arm when she slipped on some damp leaves. The sun was up, and the waterfall glistened beneath the natural stone bridge carved by centuries of running water. A bird sang. Matt was smiling, but inside her head Kay heard him crying and yelling the night he'd returned to the van. She'd known as soon as she saw the radio and the red sweater. Caroline's sweater, with blood drying stiff on the sleeves.

In the motor home, she searched mechanically for a coffeepot while Matt folded his blanket and laid it neatly at the foot of the couch. *Like prison,* she thought. She ran water in an electric coffee maker and measured coffee into the basket. *"I brought you tea, Mama."* Jeff needed liquids to bring down his fever. Now that Matt was happy, he'd relax his guard. She'd tell someone about Jeff, send help before—

Matt wandered around the room humming softly. She plugged in the coffeepot, not letting her mind dwell on the woman who had bought it and used it. Crackling sound filled the motor home and she whirled. Static. A radio. Like before—Again, memory saturated her.

* * *

"Police have intensified the manhunt for two teenage killers after the brutal slaying of a couple and their two children at Bridge Bay campground of Yellowstone Park. Matt Briggs and Kathy Gerrett of Blue Canyon, Oregon, have been positively identified as the pair who have left eight dead in a murder spree that has shocked the nation. The first victims, Kathy Gerrett's father and five-year-old brother, were found brutally butchered in their farm home three days ago when school officials investigated the Gerrett girl's absence. It's believed she and Briggs are driving a white van stolen from a feed store where Briggs was employed as a delivery boy. The van has been connected to two other murders in Idaho and Montana as well as the most recent crime in Yellowstone. Police and the FBI have thrown a dragnet around the Yellowstone area—"

Matt had driven all night while she huddled in the back of the van in darkness and terror. *"You killed them—you killed them—"*

Matt snapped off the radio impatiently. "It's the mountains," he said knowingly.

Kay opened a cupboard and found ceramic mugs with *Grandpa* and *Grandma* stenciled on them. She wondered how old the grandchildren were. She put the mugs on the table as Matt sat down at the table, smiling. His world was right. His fantasy world. Kay turned back to watch the coffee perk. Was Jeff warm enough? She should have buttoned the mackinaw. A faint flutter of movement drew her glance to the windshield. The sun playing on the pines? No, there it was again—She made herself look back at the coffeepot when she realized Matt was watching her.

"We're gonna see Old Faithful first," he said. "Do you know there's hundreds of geysers? They built a wooden path so you can walk out in this place where these things bubble and steam. Pretty colors. Some of them are deep.

They ain't never found out how deep. Sometimes people try to get close and fall in and they never find the bodies.''

She let her gaze slide across the window as she looked at him, but the shadows had settled.

"Hey, ain't that coffee done? I'm starved. You suppose there's anything to eat?''

She opened the refrigerator. "Eggs, bacon, bread.'' It was fully stocked, ready for a camping trip that Grandpa and Grandma would never take.

"Fix some.''

She moved the coffeepot. Little puffs of steam rose from the spout. Like Old Faithful.

"How many eggs do you want?''

"Three. No, four. I can have all I want now.'' He laughed happily.

Kay found a frying pan and laid strips of bacon in it. She lit the burner. When the shadows outside the window moved again, her skin crawled. Something tapped the side of the motor home.

"What was that?'' Matt leaned toward the window.

"What?''

"I heard something—''

"It's just the bacon. How do you want your eggs?'' She rattled the plates and silverware. "Scrambled? Remember that morning we ate in the cafe in that little town? I didn't even know how to order. I was so excited about eating in a restaurant.''

He turned back solemnly. "We'll eat in lots of restaurants, Katie. You can have anything you want. I'll get you everything. Just tell me and it's yours.''

She forced a smile. "I'll have to think about it. Right now, all I want is breakfast. The bacon smells delicious. It makes my mouth water.''

There it was again. Something had definitely moved out there. She heard a faint whisper of grass. Or was it the bacon sizzling? She fixed her gaze on the stove. Had Matt locked the door? She tried to remember if she'd heard the latch click.

Did the park rangers check the roads every morning? It was against the rules to park like this. What had Matt done with the knife? She glanced toward the table.

Outside—a figure—oh, God—Someone was there! The glimpse of tan vanished. But she'd seen it, she'd seen it! She unplugged the coffeepot and carried it to the table, filling the mugs. Matt cupped his hands around one and raised it.

"I bet you're a good cook, Katie. Can you make spaghetti? That's my favorite. Juhnny used to laugh. He said everyone should like steak and potatoes best."

She glanced sidelong at the window. Where was he? *Oh, God, don't let him leave. I have to tell him about Jeff—*"I like spaghetti too." She tried to laugh but it was a brittle sound that made Matt look up. "I cook it with mushrooms and black olives and lots of onions—" The door handle moved. "Do you like garlic bread with it?" she said desperately.

"Hey, the bacon's burning!" Matt yelled.

"Oh—" She set down the coffeepot and lifted the frying pan from the burner. Behind her, the door banged open.

"Don't move!" A uniformed park ranger aimed a gun through the opening.

Matt dived from the chair. He was holding the knife as though he'd never let go of it. He sprang as the ranger fired, leading with the knife and coming in low like a slithering reptile. The shot went wild. The bullet ricocheted off the refrigerator to embed itself in the back of the driver's seat. The ranger tried to jump back, but the blade caught him in the midsection. He staggered and collapsed. The gun thudded to the ground. Breath hissing, Matt crawled sideways and crouched in the space beside the stairwell.

Suddenly Elliot was there, lunging for the gun. As Matt tensed, ready to spring, Kay hurled the frying pan. The hot grease spattered Matt's face and soaked through his shirt. He screamed and covered his eyes. The knife clattered to the steps. Elliot grabbed for it, but Matt's groping hand found it first and he slashed out blindly. It caught Elliot's cheek, and a red line snaked across his face. With a desperate thrust, he grabbed Matt and yanked him outside. They tumbled to the frosty ground and struggled in the dust.

Sobbing, Kay crept down the steps. The knife blade gleamed wickedly in a shaft of early morning sun. Elliot clutched Matt's arm in a desperate effort to prevent the knife from finding its target as they thrashed. Crazed, Matt tore loose and stabbed viciously, but Elliot bucked like a bronco and threw him off balance. The knife scraped the hard ground. Matt rolled onto Elliot and braced an arm across his throat. Straddling him, Matt raised the knife again.

Kay's vision blurred. Matt Briggs had destroyed her life once. She couldn't let him do it again. He'd already terrified and abused Jeff . . . and now he was going to kill Elliot . . . Shaking, she sank to the step of the motor home and picked up the ranger's gun. It seemed an eternity until she had it gripped in both hands and aimed at Matt's thin back. She pulled the trigger when the knife in Matt's upraised hand began to plunge toward Elliot. The shot splintered the morning stillness.

The knife flew from Matt's hand as he grabbed his shoulder. Bright blood spurted between his fingers and across the plaid shirt. With a savage kick that left Elliot gasping for breath, Matt sprang at Kay. For a moment, she saw only his outstretched, bloody hand.

Red . . . blood-red . . . Her hysterical scream filled the air.

From both sides of the clearing, rangers sprang with guns drawn. Whirling, Matt wrenched the gun from Kay's limp hands and fired blindly. Shots answered from both ends of the motor home.

Matt jerked, twisting in agony as he fell, then lay still. Elliot crawled past him to take Kay in his arms.

44

"The doctor says Kay's still delirious, but the fever's coming down," Elliot said. Jeff, too, was responding to antibiotics, and the pediatrician had pronounced him out of danger.

Harriet sank into the blue Naugahyde waiting-room chair. "Has she said anything?"

Elliot wiped away his tears without shame. "She keeps saying it wasn't her fault."

"Of course it wasn't!"

Elliot gave a wry laugh. "Not about Briggs. Her mother. All these years she's been carrying guilt she didn't deserve. Her father let her believe her mother died because she hadn't gotten help fast enough."

"Love and guilt can be dreadful burdens when you can't separate them."

"I'm going to make sure she and Jeff don't hang on to any guilt this time. We're all going to a counselor as soon as they're well. No more ghosts."

Harriet squeezed his hand. "Too bad Briggs never got help," she said. "Farmington was here. The prison authorities say Briggs's escape was precipitated by the death of the one friend he had inside, a lifer named Clark Juhn, who had the cell next to him. They spent a lot of time together. Juhn worked in the prison library and got Briggs interested in reading and studying. He also spent a lot of time in Yellowstone and this area. When he died, Briggs went to pieces"

"So he escaped and made for the one other person he ever loved." Elliot wanted to feel rage, but it wouldn't come. Matt Briggs was dead. *Love and guilt and the whole damned thing,* he thought. *Kay suppressed hers. Briggs clung to his.*

A nurse came out of Kay's room. "You can go in now, Mr. Pier."

Elliot jumped up. "Is she—?"

"She's conscious and asking for you."

Harriet squeezed his hand. "I'll go sit with Jeff."

Elliot went into the room and stood by the bed. Kay smiled weakly as he bent to kiss her. He took her hand.

"It's over, sweetheart," he said. "Jeff's doing fine, you're doing fine. Everything's going to be all right."

"What about—?"

"Don't think about that now." He kissed her again, giving her his strength. "Think about getting well so the three of us can go home."

Kay pressed his hand. Her eyes closed and her breath fluttered. When she looked at him again, there was a smile in her eyes. He leaned close to hear her words. "I was going to ask, what about your book? What did Trevor say?"

Elliot started to laugh, hugging her. "I left before he read it. I want us to be together when I hear the news."

"I'll stock up on champagne. We're going to have a lot to celebrate."

He nodded. A lot to celebrate.